DIVIDED WE FELL

The Divided America Zombie Apocalypse
Book One

B. D. Lutz

ACKNOWLEDGEMENTS

Edited by Monique Happy Editorial Services
www.moniquehappyeditorial.com

Thank you for your hard work and
guidance. But most of all, thank you for
answering a random email from a newbie. This
wouldn't have happened without you!

Cover designed by: Kelly A. Martin
www.kam.design

Kelly, the Louvre called and they
want their art back. I told them no!

Photography by benkrut (DepositPhotos)
Mppriv (DepositPhotos)
chagpg (DepositPhotos)

PROLOGUE

"Now is our time to strike the imperialists, to crush them," First Vice Chairman, Choke proclaimed while bowing his head in respect of Dear Leader. "Any resistance in Blue States United will be easily destroyed. We start with New York City. They have few weapons, a pathetic military, and no armed citizens."

He raised his head and referred to the retractable projector screen displaying a hand-drawn image of New York City with Times Square highlighted in red. He changed the slide on the 1950s-era overhead projector to show a drawing of LA with Interstate 405 highlighted and said, "We finish with Los Angeles."

He placed a fresh slide on the projector with the population statistics for New York. The slide was simple, yet brought stillness to the room. It read: "Population Density: New York 28,000 people per square mile. Population Density: Manhattan 72,000 people per square mile." Before he could place the slide with Los Angeles' population, Vice Chairman Packet interjected, "Have we fully tested the weapon? Do you understand the trajectory of its devastation?"

FVC Choke, visibly annoyed by the interruption, cut a hard glare at Packet and said, "It has been tested enough to know it will bring America to its knees. They will beg Dear Leader for mercy."

Choke was an experienced and vicious politician. He had navigated the deadly world of Dear Leader's politics successfully for years and knew his statement would solidify his plan. Dear Leader wouldn't allow the opportunity to crush the West to dirt slip by.

"It is settled, we move by the end of the week. No more waiting or delays, NOW." The little leader slammed his hand on his highly polished desk and ordered the meeting to an end.

In a moment of weak self control, VC Packet blurted out, "Dear Leader, do we have the arrangement with our Blue States United operatives finalized?" He needn't see Dear Leader's face. He knew the look being cast upon him. He dropped his eyes to the plush carpet and began mumbling an apology, when he was cut short.

"Packet, you question me? You question my supreme knowledge of the world? You want our great country to wait for permission from dotards?" The room was silent as Dear Leader glared at his cabinet member.

FVC Choke understood what was happening; Dear Leader was trying to determine how to end Packet's life.

"No, Dear Leader, I respect all of your glorious power and supreme knowledge. I merely felt it wise to ensure they honor the pact. The Committee to Reunite..."

He again was cut short and recognized his deadly mistake as Dear Leader screamed, "I am the wisest of all." He paused, soaking up the fear in the room, before continuing, "VC Packet, you will join me in my quarters after my medical team has completed their tasks."

Packet stood with his hands folded at his waist and realized he still held the glass vial containing the sample of the weapon Choke had passed out. An idea worthy of his corrupted soul rushed at him. He forced tears down his cheeks; it was expected, not an honest display of his emotional state.

Dear Leader turned abruptly and exited the room. Packet only hoped the intensity of the moment would allow the sample to be forgotten.

Choke approached him as Packet's heart pounded. "It was good working with you, VC Packet. I wish for you to live long enough to witness our destruction of the West. I will miss you." Choke gave a quick bow and exited with the other cabinet members.

Relief eased the tension in Packet's shoulders as he held the vial in the palm of his hand. He heard the medical cart approaching and moved to the door to let them enter through the office adjoining Dear Leader's private quarters.

The armed escort, intimidated by Packet's presence, stopped at the door to stand guard. Mustering up his most commanding voice, he ordered the nurse to stop as she crossed the threshold and shut the door behind her.

"Dear Leader requires his medicine be inspected." The questioning gaze from the nurse prompted a response that slithered like a snake from his mouth, "Please, feel free to *question* Dear Leader's direction. He is waiting in his quarters."

The fear that flashed across her face told Packet he had control, but he needed to move quickly. The nurse backed away from the tray that held Dear Leader's *medicine*. Packet opened the vial containing the weapon and set it on the tray next to the containers of white powder. *You are nothing but a dope-head that should be living on the streets of America*, he thought as he mixed the two powders together. He feigned interest in the mixture, as if waiting for an explosion of activity to erupt from the powder resting on the silver tray, next to the hypodermic.

The young nurse watched intently, knowing her life depended on the outcome of the lab experiment happening in front of her. Packet, with sweat coating his hands, looked at the young woman and nodded. He poured the mixture into the *medicine* container and placed the remainder back into the glass vial.

"Please hurry," he said, "Dear Leader needs his medicine, quickly. Go, go now."

Packet sat in Choke's chair and placed the deadly combination next to the man's empty drinking glass. He leaned back and waited for his end to come.

A smile creased his reptilian features as the nurse exited the private quarters and he was summoned.

CHAPTER 1:
MY NAME IS OTTO

The Great Divide happened two years and three months ago. Something most humans never thought possible.

We now call it the Split, and it's the reason all of this happened. It's the reason I'm holed up in a basement of an abandoned house, sweating my butt off with five other people. Each of us hoping and praying they pass by, that they keep shambling to the next house or the one after that. We've been in a running battle with them for the last hour.

Our ammo is okay but not enough for a prolonged siege. Our food situation is light, and we've got enough water for two days if we're careful. However, those are the least of our concerns.

We started the day six strong and picked up two survivors near Right Entry Point One. After talking with the survivors for a few minutes, we realized something about them didn't fit. They didn't ask, they demanded... that says it all. But to remove all doubt, they had no firearms, only the most basic self-defense tools, and they appeared uncomfortable using those tools. All of that together confirmed them as being from Blue States United.

We didn't care where you called home as long as you could fight, but guess what? They couldn't fight.

We determined they wouldn't cut it because they kept working towards the middle of our group to ensure two things for themselves. The first: Avoid being forced to fight. The second: Someone with a gun would be there, protecting them. When we called them on it, they started to cry. They told us how aggressive and unfair we were being for asking them to fight these things, to fight to live. They said they weren't trained to kill, but we were.

There is no crying during the apocalypse!

The herd latched onto us while we made our way back to our vehicle. We turned down the wrong street, and they poured out of the buildings that lined it.

The buildings and abandoned cars made the street tight, and they converged on our position in a matter of seconds.

Our fighting moved from rifles to handguns to pure hand to hand combat in a matter of minutes. The first of the herd to break through our rolling defensive perimeter used to be a young man of about eighteen. Someone had pummelled him, breaking every bone in his face, but he still shambled our way.

Randy used his rifle stock to knock it to the ground and stomped what remained of its face into something resembling meat pudding... is that a thing?

That started what became the longest hour of my life. They came from everywhere! Stumbling from doorways or broken windows, alleys and fire escapes, you name the opening and they found a way through it.

They moved slowly but relentlessly; never fatigued, always on the hunt. They simply never stopped. We needed to find cover to catch our breath, hydrate, and come up with a strategy.

Communication to our extraction support was cut off due to interference and poor training on the radio we'd been issued. We needed cover, now!

We determined this house, the house we'd inadvertently trapped ourselves in, was our best option. Randy and I would breach the door and cover the approach of the team. We ALL agreed to the plan before we even got close to the house. Randy and I would neutralize any initial threats leaving a clear path for the team. They would move single file as quickly as possible, with the survivors in the middle of the line.

However, to avoid anything that resembled danger during the charge to the house, the survivors fell back... too far back. One significant problem with their plan. The team moved fast, faster than they'd expected. They quickly lost the cover they had been using to stay safe and walked directly into the arms of the throng. How they lost their situational awareness was beyond me, and I never had the chance to ask them. It cost them their lives, and that's the reality of it.

Their lives ended quick and loud. The first to die didn't even see it coming, and the shock in his eyes turned to terror in a flash. He started to scream, but one of the things stuck its hand into his mouth, cutting off his pleas just as it clamped its mouth onto his neck. The bite sent blood spraying into the air and down his shirt as it wrenched his lower jaw off. When his jaw broke free, with tendons and muscles clinging to bone, I thought about chicken wings with thick, sweet BBQ sauce. Suddenly I got sad that I'd never eat another wing or go to a wing night ever again. Don't judge me.

The monster that caused the initial damage looked like a truck had run it over and accelerated on its midsection. The thing's insides were scooped out, leaving an empty cavern where its stomach and intestines should have been. It sounds nasty, but I still wanted some wings.

The other survivor disappeared under the mass of undead, letting loose a brutal scream until the crush of bodies silenced her.

We had already entered the house as they ripped her apart, but that scream traveled for miles, drawing more monsters to her, allowing us time to secure the door and find the basement.

The main floor had too many access points to cover, and we hoped they would lose track of us and, in turn, lose interest and move on. The basement was our best option.

I'm not upset they're gone. If that seems cold, it is. This new reality is hard, and you can't get bogged down with feelings for those who won't fight to live. I hadn't even bothered to learn their names.

So, here we sit. Me and Will, Randy and Stone, Jax and Lisa, in a musty, stinky basement filled with boxes of the nastiest smelling food I have ever come across in my life. The food resembled someone's attempt at making a sausage of some sort, and their attempt had failed miserably.

By the way, my name is Otto.

CHAPTER 2:
TIME IN THE SQUARE

The smell of eggs, bacon, and coffee made Adam smile as he stirred in his comfy bed. Beth was working her magic in the kitchen.

The intoxicating aroma made his stomach growl as he envisioned the table in their Manhattan apartment, occupying the corner of Broad and Exchange Place, filled with her handiwork. Bacon just crisp enough, eggs over easy with a dash of salt and two of pepper, and that coffee she made was better than anyplace in the city. He never told her about his morning stops at Benny's; that coffee was for effect. Hers was for taste.

As he resisted opening his eyes to start his morning as the CEO of Broad View Marketing, he noticed the sickly-sweet stench of rot seeping in around the corners of Beth's breakfast. He'd need to call the building super about it when he got to the office. With what this apartment cost, he shouldn't have to deal with the outside world leaching into his home.

Stretching the length of his body, he prepared himself to join the day. When his eyes opened, reality crashed in. Adam tried to close his eyes and go back to sleep; go back to Beth, to his apartment, his high-powered position. He was

Adam "The Ad-Man" Barton, not a hopeless addict. Not the man sleeping in trash behind Benny's Deli. It was just a nightmare; he'd wake from it in a moment. He stitched his eyes tight, wishing the horror of his reality away.

A familiar soothing baritone voice called out to him, "Mr. Ad-Man, got your coffee for you. But you gotta get up. You slept in today. Benny will have a fit he finds you here this late."

Tears flooded Adam's eyes as he realized he'd again lost the fight to stay in his previous life. He bolted upright and faced his old friend. Tyler had worked at Benny's back when Adam was on top of his game. When his life was good and whole.

Tyler had his coffee ready for him every day as Adam walked to his office. On days Adam ran late, Tyler would have it waiting on the counter so Adam didn't have to wait in line. Tyler was a good man and never stopped getting his coffee ready for him. Even after his life fell apart, he got Adam his coffee.

"I can't bring you any food this morning. Stop back later, after the morning rush, I'll have something for you then."

Tyler looked at his friend sitting atop the large piece of cardboard resting on a heap of yesterday's trash. "You get to that clinic I told you about? They helped me, Adam, they can help you."

He wiped away his tears and reached with grimy hands for the coffee his friend held. "I'm going today." Eyes shifting rapidly as he thought of his next lie. "I'm going to undo what the doctors did to me. But man, my back hurts. I need something for the pain."

Tyler shook his head. The conversation went the same way every morning. "Adam, *you* got to *undo* a lot of things. First, undo your thinking about who put you here.

"Remember, if you find yourself at the clinic, ask for Jessica. I told her about you; she's looking forward to meeting you. Now, get gone before Benny finds you and fires me."

Adam stood on cramped legs and started off. He had to get to his corner before Alex set up on it. He stopped and turned to ask his friend, "You seen Rudy or Ezek around? I haven't seen them since they were talking to a couple of Asian fellas night before last. Rudy lost his corner to that prick Stan. Mean SOB that one."

Tyler addressed him over his shoulder, "Come to think of it, I haven't. Stay away from those Asian guys; they just showed up and I don't like the looks of them." With that, the back door to Benny's slammed shut. The noise echoed in the alley, reminding Adam that he was still alone in the world.

"I miss you, Beth."

He beat Alex to his corner by less than a minute and set up shop. He chugged the last of the coffee and dried the cup with grimy shirttails, then placed it on the sidewalk it in front of him. Opening his filth-covered, full-length overcoat revealed his handmade sign, the sign that now defined his life.

Homeless Please Help. God Bless.

He knew the shame would pass after he collected enough money for his medicine. He'd be *even* in just a few hours. His mouth watered at the thought.

The morning rush was profitable. His corner was where Wall Street, Beaver Street and Pearl Street converged. Best corner he'd ever worked!

He hid behind a dumpster, just off Pearl, and counted his earnings. One hundred and seventy dollars. His body tingled when he thought about his medicine. He had more than enough for his daily *prescription*. He might even be able to buy some food today. Off to find the dope woman!

He walked down Pearl headed for the Broad Street subway entrance. Donna would have his first dose of medicine waiting for him. It looked like a good day ahead!

At the corner of Pearl and Hanover he spotted one of the Asians he'd been seeing. He loomed on the opposite corner, seemingly waiting for Adam to cross.

The slight and vertically challenged man stood out, dressed in a black suit with dark sunglasses. But the thing that truly identified him was his lack of movement. The bustling crowds passed by the man in every direction as he stood motionless, watching Adam.

He needed his medicine and had no time for games. Adam crossed the street, giving the man in the black suit a wide berth.

The man called out to him by name, with a strong accent. *"You come here, Adam. We have food and medicine from Donna."*

The last part stopped him cold. How did he know about Donna? Why would she give them Adam's medicine? He was already sweating and needed his meds. This game wasn't going to work.

He turned hard in Black-Suit's direction and said, "How do you know my name? Why do you have my medicine?" Adam's hands trembled as perspiration flowed down his body. *God, don't let this happen, I need my meds.*

The man talked into his shoulder and a flash later a shuttle-style bus pulled next to Adam. The door opened and he saw Rudy's smiling face. He sat on a plush bench seat. He looked good; he looked *even*.

"Adam, get in. It's a damn party on wheels in here." Rudy said, grinning through rotten teeth.

Adam approached the bus, happy to see his friend but still uneasy with how events were unfolding.

Rudy said, "Adam, they have Donna's stash, all of it. We've been eating and drinking and *floating* for the last twenty-eight hours. Get in, it's like God sent this to us."

Rudy held up a baggie of white powder and Adam got on the bus, smiling ear to ear. His medicine had arrived!

Adam woke to the sound of a car horn with no memories of the previous night. He glanced around, finding Rudy next to him sleeping on torn-open hot-slimy trash bags. The smell made him gag. Like decomposed flesh.

He scrambled to Rudy and shook him violently. If they were caught in the middle of Times Square, they'd spend the day in jail. Adam had no time for jail, he needed more of the prior night's medicine. He had never soared like that in his life. Rudy didn't move. He must be deep-out of it, Adam thought.

As he sat looking at his friend, something stirred in his belly. He watched blood pump through the veins in Rudy's neck and it did something to him. Something he didn't understand, something that scared him. It made him hungry, so hungry.

Rudy's eyes fluttered, and he looked up at Adam, a smile pushing through the muck on his face. Rudy said, "I told you, ain't that the best shit you ever pushed? And the food, so much food!"

He looked around, confusion lining his face, and said, "Adam, where's the bus, why are we in Times Square? We're going to get arrested. Where's Ezek?"

He started to rise when a warm liquid hit his cheek. He glanced at Adam and said, "What the hell, man? Why you spitting on me?"

Adam tilted his head and said, "Don't worry, Rudy, its only drool."

The last thing Adam remembered was Rudy's warm life's blood gushing down his throat as his friend screamed for help.

Chapter 3:
Split

After our final presidential election as the United States, how divided our country had grown over the last eight years became painfully obvious. The "movement" exposed how intolerant the tolerant really were. Physical violence started during campaign season and intensified after the election.

Mobs of enraged protesters took to blocking roads and highways, screaming in your face and being offended by your existence. Victimhood became something of a pastime for them, and WOW were they good at it.

Everyone that didn't think like them earned the label *phobic*. Name the *phobic* and that's the label you received, justified or not. They created new *phobias* and passed them out like bite-sized Snickers on Trick or Treat. So many good people lost their jobs and more for expressing different beliefs; not being or acting hateful but for *believing* differently.

The violence quickly escalated in both intensity and frequency. Before long, entire groups of people pulled together to form "protection clubs" based on ideologies or belief systems. Predictably some morphed into gang-like organizations going on the offensive more often than not.

Our political system ground to a halt. Each side had dug in for the fight and no one wanted to compromise. NO ONE.

Family units crumbled and friendships splintered, sometimes with devastating consequences. We heard stories of families being brutalized by protection clubs (also known as PCs) after one of the family members complained to the club about their family's beliefs. Sometimes for simply saying something the PC didn't like. People got hurt, some killed, all for believing differently than even one of their family members.

Thinking back, I can see how We The People drew the battle lines long before our politicians pushed us off the cliff.

Our politicians exploited our division with skillful manipulation, absence of morality, or any thought of the consequences. *America be damned, I'm keeping my job... my power.*

Then it happened! Something I never imagined possible. Americans voted to determine which "America" your state would align with. You can re-read that as many times as you'd like, but it won't change. The American people voted to become a red or blue state. The outcome would place your state under Conservative leadership or Liberal rule.

As fans of the Constitution it was an easy choice; we voted Conservative. Unsurprisingly, America voted as it did in the last presidential election, shocking the shit out of Democrats, again. I'm not sure why. Most people like the Constitution and let it guide their choice.

They completed the Split six months after the vote, and none of the doomsday predictions came true. Now, I'm not saying it was easy. A lot of families pulled up roots and moved to the America best suited for them. It created much turmoil and hardship for some and opportunity for others.

Soon afterwards, a group of BSU companies conspired to boycott Right America (RAM), realizing quickly they needed flyover country. And only selling to individuals they deemed "worthy" of their products while turning a profit wasn't possible. I loved that part.

Hollywood learned the same lesson. It takes more than people living on the East and West Coasts, to make money. Or at least the amounts of money they earned before the Split.

BSU made its expected moves. They outlawed firearms for civilians, cut the military to the equivalent of a protection force, and struggled to fill the boots for that force. They hamstrung the police and inevitably crime spiked in all major cities. That forced more people from BSU to RAM.

I will say the move by BSU to cut the military was a brilliant strategy. They knew RAM wouldn't allow a hostile country at its border, and that we would defend them to stop that from happening.

However, they didn't expect to receive a bill for that

service. When they pushed back on paying and refused to implement any immigration control, RAM built a border wall between RAM and BSU. It utilized the most ingenious access technology ever envisioned, and it worked like a charm. Any challenges to Commerce were addressed and quickly remedied.

Starting at one mile from an entry point, vehicles, including semi and cargo trucks, traversed three separate drive-through, multi-view x-ray units. In addition to the x-ray views, each unit came equipped with additional technologies. The first unit employed air-sniffers tuned for explosives capable of detecting a single molecule of numerous explosive materials. The second sniffer searched for a wide spectrum of chemical agents in gas or liquid form. The third unit searched for illegal drugs.

The entry lanes were divided into passenger and cargo traffic with all lanes employing the technology. The semi and cargo truck lanes used RFID readers that linked back to the cargo manifest which was transmitted prior to the truck's arrival at the gate. RFID identified everything about the shipment, down to its value for taxation purposes. Ohhh yes, taxation remained alive and well on both sides. Politicians always found a way to stick their hands in our pockets... legalized theft is what I called it.

Any vehicle that failed the inspections got diverted to a secondary screening area that was set up for the specific test they failed. Of course, all vehicles and persons entering RAM needed to be registered (AKA a passport). The registration data fed a facial recognition system capable of scanning hundreds of faces per-minute. If you planned on entering RAM, that software better recognize your mug or you were diverted.

Foot traffic was subjected to similar scrutiny, just on a smaller scale. After the access technologies were deployed, foot traffic declined nearly sixty percent. It's amazing what a good deterrent can accomplish.

The wall, past the entry points, was a behemoth that extended twenty-two feet in the air and fourteen feet below the surface. The depth served two purposes. First, it made the wall difficult to tunnel under. Second, it severed all the utility and water lines that ran between RAM and BSU, forcing BSU to become self-sufficient. Seems they forgot how much infrastructure depended on RAM supply lines.

The wall was a steel-bollard construction style with flat steel panels attached at a height of fifteen feet. The construction severely limited one's ability to scale or pass through the wall but allowed our patrols visibility to the other side. Coupled with regular patrols and the strategic use of drones, the number of illegal crossings dropped dramatically.

In retrospect, that wall helped Right America slow the spread of the virus and is the reason RAM is in a much stronger position today.

The Split held more surprises for BSU. For instance, the volume of people preferring to live in RAM. Not so much the number, but the diversity of people who made the choice. They found out what we already knew: We are not the horrible people they were told we were. We want everyone to live the long-thought-dead American Dream.

Now, do we have our problems? Yes. However, the world discovered that the trash BSU had been peddling was true hate. When BSU ran out of politicians and groups to blame it laid bare how hateful and intolerant they were as they turned on each other.

And, of course, I still find plenty of things I disagree with in RAM's political system. But that's how I work. I really don't like government as a whole. For years I voted for the liar whose values and message aligned the closest to mine. They always disappointed me. But in RAM we talk these things out, mostly avoiding the crazy screaming and temper tantrums that, for years, defined our politics.

Chapter 4:
The 405

One of LAPD's finest loomed over Wild as he sat on the sidewalk in the boiling mid-day sun. Wild couldn't tell if the officer, reviewing his *papers*, was looking at him from behind his blackout sunglasses, and didn't care. He waited for the question he knew was coming.

"Who the hell names their kid Wild William Williamson?" the officer asked.

Right again, Wild thought. He shrugged off the question and said, "My *papers* are valid. Give 'em back."

The officer glanced around the area to ensure he hadn't walked into another ambush. Then he said, "I have to run your ID, Wild. Remain seated." The officer retreated to the interior of the AC-cooled patrol car leaving Wild to bake on the corner of Burbank and The 405.

He was less than two hundred yards from the shade of his tent in the Sepulveda Basin encampment. He needed a nap. The *Hell Dust* those Asians were slinging was the shit. It slammed him last night and would do the same again tonight. The dumb sons-a-bitches were extending credit to the entire camp.

The chemically enhanced physique of the officer

unfolded from the black and white. "You're free to go, Mr. Williamson. Stop pissing in public, understand?" He handed Wild his ID and the obligatory *Homeless Advocacy Information* pamphlet.

Wild handed it back to the officer and said, "Keep it. Those bastards can't handle Wild Bill. And the food sucks." He jumped to his feet and headed for *home*.

He hit the basin and took a hard left towards his tent. Vicky would be waiting and pissed that he'd come home with no *candy*. He was thirty feet from his front door when the little man in black stepped from behind Nathan's tin home, the nicest house in the camp. Rich bastard.

Wild's eyes lit up when he saw the dope-man. Wild's mouth was moving before his brain told him to shut up. "How's the English, any better?" He grimaced at his words and tried to rebound and preserve his line of credit. "No worries, brother, we're all the same under our skin." He had no idea why he'd referenced the man's color when he had insulted his accent. "We all bleed red, right?" With his head in his hands, he thought, *Wild, shut your stupid mouth. It's why you live in a tent with a prostitute.*

The wisp of a man slid a hand inside his two-sizes-too-big suit jacket. The action didn't escape Wild. Hands in supplication, he said, "Whoa, that wasn't a threat. I have issues. I'm a sick prick that can't shut his head or mouth off. No reason to kill a mentally ill man."

A sticky smile broke the man's leathery tight face as his hand retreated from inside his jacket. "You a funny man, Mr. Weird."

Wild stifled a laugh and said, "Just call me Bob."

The Asian dope-man nodded and said, "You come with me now, Bob. I have what you and your rady friend need. We have fun night. Food too."

Head cocked, Wild said, "Rady friend? Ooooh, you mean Vicky, my *lady* friend. Food, dope, and my money maker? Let's go."

Thirty minutes later, Wild took his last breath.

"It is done, First Vice Chair Choke. We will drop the final two on the motorway in three minutes. They received the weapon thirty-seven minutes ago. DPRK now has forty weapons on the motorway 405, three more than our counterparts in New York. Please send our tickets for our return home."

Choke ignored the request and said, "Dear Leader is most exuberant. You have served the DPRK with honor. Children will sing of your accomplishments."

Chest swelling the man said, "Our names on Dear Leader's lips brings great joy. We will join the children in singing the glory of Dear Leader. We would like to be home soonest." The man received no reply to his second request to come home. He checked the LCD screen on his encrypted phone to confirm he was still connected to FVC Choke. He was.

Choke said, "We have made a decision that will leave you supremely happy. You will remain to ensure our weapons find their targets." Choke was greeted with silence. His temper flared at the insubordination. They should thank him for allowing them to fight longer. They should be honored that he trusted them to die for the DPRK if need be.

He prepared to remind them that their families, who were still being *cared for* by Dear Leader's personal guards, would be most disappointed in them. His mouth hinged opened when a muffled voice, speaking English, said, "Bob, you go back to your rady friend."

Choke began calculating the time, panic overtaking his armored emotions. It was too soon.

"BOB, sit down or—" A scream cut the agent's sentence off.

Something was wrong. Had the weapons revolted? Choke held the phone tight and screamed for a response. The line was dead.

He ran to the secured monitor that had been scanning local channels in New York and Los Angeles. He flipped through screens, his heart pounding when the monitor stopped on the breaking news alert from News 7 LA. Hundreds of weapons ran lose on the motorway, but something was wrong. They moved like cripples, not the stealthy and aggressive attackers the weapon should have transformed them into.

As the aerial view panned along the motorway, it rested on an image of a small bus flipped on its side. Its position on the motorway blocked two of the five lanes. Two men dressed in black struggled to exit the twisted vehicle. As a police car approached in the berm, Choke watched in horror as one of his agents scrambled from the wreckage, kneeled in front of the police car and put his hands in the air.

Choke swept the monitor from the table, crashing it to the marble floor. They had failed and he would soon be dead because of it. His rampage was cut short when a woman's bloodcurdling scream reached him through an open window.

Choke held tight to the window frame to support his girth as his knees buckled at the sight of a young Traffic Lady being pulled to the ground and torn to pieces. He turned from the scene, searching his mind for an answer, when his phone buzzed.

Dear Leader was calling.

Chapter 5:
Reflection

While we sat, guarding the entrances to the basement and listening to the thumping and shuffling of the monsters surrounding the house, I got caught up in memories of how we got here. I drifted to the day I watched the first video from Times Square on that fateful Saturday night. It took over an hour before anyone realized the homeless were attacking people, using bites as their weapons. The ensuing chaos and how the media swarmed the area, looking for the mass-shooting, after the sound of gunshots ringing out were reported, still awed me.

I recalled that while our attention was drawn to New York, LA was hit. Again, the exceedingly large homeless population was the weapon of choice. They were set loose on The 405 at rush hour. I remembered thinking, *LA's freeways at rush hour, or any other time of day, are the world's largest parking lots. Those poor people were virtually trapped on the freeway.*

It was hideous. The videos showed the ease with which the homeless walked up and down the rows of cars, biting unsuspecting drivers or smashing windows to get to the food inside. The amount of infected after that attack was staggering. But no one knew what it meant or how bad it would get.

RAM intelligence later *discovered* the interrogation videos of the two DPRK agents captured by the BSU. They revealed the grim reality that North Korea had unleashed this hell on us.

The CDC determined that the virus was intended to be a virulent form of influenza combined with the hemorrhagic Marburg virus and several other nasty little bugs. The other bugs ensured it would mutate every time we introduced an effective vaccine or cure. In other words, they designed it to kill in the most horrific way imaginable while spreading fear and chaos across the country, or so the CDC thought.

Unfortunately, it seemed, they'd never tested the *vessels* they'd planned to use. The drug-addled systems of the homeless caused it to mutate in a way that was unforeseen. I'm confident the DPRK didn't set out to bring the world to the brink of extinction; they just wanted to crush the U.S. But what do you expect from North Korea? The little madman and his minions were in such a rush to be the first to hit us, they couldn't be bothered with silly testing.

And well, here we are, hiding from several hundred zombies in a basement. Yes, I said zombies. We've been calling them *things*, but I want to be clear with you what we're fighting: living dead, Zs, zombies, or things. Call them what you will, they are real, and they are hungry.

North Korea's failure to conduct proper testing not

only contributed to the reanimation mutation, it caused the development of slow- and fast-acting versions of the virus.

The fast-acting version took effect within a few minutes to several days of the person being bitten. The slow version could take a week to turn the infected person, allowing it to spread around the world.

After being treated for bites, and before we understood the implications, tens of thousands of people caught flights, got on ships, or drove to other states and across the borders of other countries. They felt fine when they arrived at their destination, but not much longer after. By the time we understood what hit us, it had become a worldwide extinction-level event.

As they turned, they died, and died in a way that drew people to them. People trying to help them. We're talking convulsions, passing out, hitting the ground and drawing attention, and their victims, to them. When they came back, they attacked anyone within biting range.

We lost so many first responders in the days after the virus hit that we barely had enough of them to keep things going. BSU hit an eighty-seven percent first responder casualty rate in the first week. No matter how many times the first responders asked for armed escorts, the politicians refused. *We don't need guns; we need compassion!* one stretched-face House Rep shouted from inside the safe confines of her gated home.

The images being broadcast, after the first attacks,

showed some horrific scenes unfolding in everyday American cities. Because gunfire usually accompanied the scenes, as with the first attacks, the media moved with haste, calling it a *wave of gun violence*. This tactic further confused the situation and caused people to react far too slowly.

Witnesses reported gunshots and wounded *victims* becoming disoriented and biting first responders. The dramas ended with the first responders shooting the victims. So, they ran with gun violence.

Side note: I'm an avid zombie-novel reader. So after the real news got out, it took me about thirty seconds to put the pieces together. Maybe twenty-six seconds, but you get the point.

I loaded all the magazines for all of our firearms and had the ready bags, well, ready to go. I placed our firearms in strategic locations around the house, readily available for use. I completed this in less than seven minutes. Yes, I timed it. We have a six-foot-high fence around our backyard. It's only a vinyl privacy fence, but it saved my life the first night of the outbreak. The single soft spot was the gate, standing four feet high and of the picket variety. I blocked that entrance with our Jeep. We have a detached garage, so it was imperative that the gate hold.

Sorry, I got a little distracted.

The media pounded the gun violence message, and it was getting people killed. We determined the media had been editing footage sent to them from bystanders in an effort to reinforce the gun violence message. Knowing how the news cycles work, the attacks by the homeless got pushed aside. All they talked about was gun violence.

People posted videos to YouTube and other social media platforms to spread the word. By the time it all sank in, we found ourselves knee-deep in the chaos while many areas across the country had already been fighting for their lives.

The fast-acting virus became the predominant of the two and started to "mutate" about three days into this mess. It started turning people in minutes, well before they could be dealt with properly. That rapid transformation caused chaos in the streets. People died, turned, and spread the virus.

The slow-acting version also proved exceptionally devastating in its own unique way. The delay gave people hope that the longer it took to change, the higher the chances the infected person would avoid turning. That hope got them killed. They wouldn't restrain them or post a watch to ensure that if they turned, someone could stop them from attacking others.

I can understand waiting and hoping that a miracle would happen and your loved one would pull through. However, not taking the basic precautions as communicated by the CDC and law enforcement guaranteed your death at the hands of an infected loved one. Thousands were slaughtered in their homes by people they thought would recover, feeding the ranks of the dead.

They roamed the streets like packs of wolves, slow

wolves with limited motor skills, true, but those packs proved deadly.

The strange thing was that they seemed to stay in whatever *packs* they first teamed up with. The science community theorized that a basic-level function told them it was easier to find food in a pack. I called it petrifying. If you found yourself in the middle of a pack, not ready to fight like the third monkey on the ramp to Noah's Ark, you died a horrible death.

Chapter 6:
Some Background

So, as you may have guessed, I'm a Second Amendment supporter. I guess it isn't about the Constitution now; it's more about how you felt about the Second Amendment before. The fact is, if you had a gun, you gave yourself a fighting chance in the early days of the outbreak. A gun enabled you to keep a greater distance between you and the infected. That space determined if you lived or died. Once you let yourself get within a couple of feet of them, your survivability chances dropped significantly.

That part I told you earlier? About me having the guns loaded, placed around the house, and gate blocked all in seven minutes? It isn't a joke.

After figuring out that we were losing control, I called my wife, Darline. It's pronounced Darlene, so stop with all the crazy pronunciations in your head. It's as easy as Darlene. I told her to leave work immediately and have her Sig P238 in her hand at all times. She figured I'd finally gone crazy. So I sent her a link to a YouTube video from New York's Times Square taken two days after the first attack. She opened it, watched it, and hit the road in less time than it took me to call her.

I used to joke with her about having rally points if something happened that kept us from getting home. She, in turn, called me a lunatic. However, when I called to check on her progress, she asked me which rally point to use if she got forced off of the freeway or trapped in traffic. I smiled on the inside and stored it away for reflection (AKA, something to brag about later). We talked about several places for her to jump off the freeway and to notify me immediately if she did. She hit the road at 1:15 p.m., becoming the first of us to draw blood not long after.

We live in Cleveland, Ohio. This is important because Darline would drive home on I480, a freeway that can experience some huge traffic jams. I was worried that she would drive directly into an epic tie-up and that's how it would end for her. Sitting in her car, waiting for help, or worse. I told her not to hesitate to exit the freeway if it got dicey.

Her route home took her past Cleveland Hopkins International Airport, which is visible from I480. When you see it, you're almost home with only a few stop lights in your way. Her story was the first indication of the fight ahead of us.

As she sat at the exit, a huge crowd crested the hill from the direction of the airport. Something looked wrong from the second they came into view. First, it's not normal for people to enter the freeway on foot... ever. Second, they were covered in blood.

The flash of empathy Darline felt for them disappeared

when one of them got hit by a car and thrown over the concrete divider, landing about twelve feet from her SUV. But it didn't die. It pulled itself up on mangled legs and started walking in her direction.

Several cars at the light at the bottom of the ramp halted her forward progress. She realized she'd allowed herself to be pinned in by the cars at the light and the ones on the freeway behind her.

The ramp was at a lower elevation than the actual freeway. Trees and brush flanked it to the north, and a wide shoulder and steep incline flanked it to the south. She would be forced to watch the macabre march of the fiends. The one struck by the car joined a more mobile friend and they headed in her direction. That's when she got a clear view of them and wished she hadn't.

The mobile one had been a man of about thirty; his face and chest were a mess of bites and torn skin. Something had ripped his left cheek open, exposing teeth and jaw and giving him a permanent, evil sideways grin, like a crazy joker from a ghoulish deck of playing cards. It pointed claw-like hands in her direction and held a laser focus on the line of cars.

Soon after she took in the morbid sight of the Joker-thing, the more damaged one came hobbling after. Bones and cartilage protruded through bloody rents all over his body. One foot had been ripped off at the ankle, forcing him to use it like a pirate's peg-leg.

"They should be dead; this isn't possible!" she yelled.

After breaking her trancelike stare, Darline realized no cars had moved through the light. An accident at the bottom of the exit ramp had forced them to a dead stop. Things were going off the rails fast.

Panic setting in, she turned to locate the things walking across the freeway. They had veered off their original course and now stumbled towards the car in front of her. Focused on the accident, the driver didn't notice them and made the mistake of having his windows down.

Darline realized what was about to happen and began honking her horn to get the driver's attention, but it was already too late. The Joker approached from behind the car and angled toward the driver's side window. It latched onto the man's arm, sinking its teeth into his bicep before he could react to her warning. Joined by the damaged Pirate-thing, they pulled the driver through the window, the snap of his back breaking audible in the sealed cab of her SUV.

His scream pierced the air as the things took him apart in small pieces. Then the Joker latched onto his throat, tearing it out with one bite and silencing the man forever. As they burrowed into his stomach, the Joker looked up, making eye contact with Darline. At that point she decided these things needed to die.

Darline suffered through a pang of guilt for not acting sooner. But honestly, who expects to see humans eating other humans, let alone know how to react to it?

Before she realized it, she had exited her SUV and

lined up the Pirate-thing in her P238's sights. She heard my voice in her head screaming, "HEAD SHOT" and put a round in its forehead. It was over that quick. The thing went limp, falling away from its human feast.

She started to line up the second shot, but other drivers began reacting to her gunshot. Some exited their cars to see what was happening. Others smashed through the cars surrounding them and drove to the south berm, escaping down the ramp on the grass.

She no longer had a clean shot and decided that she needed to get to safety. She also worried someone would smash her SUV. Darline loves her SUV.

As she retreated, she witnessed the Joker-thing's fetid teeth latching onto a Good Samaritan coming to aid the victim. He, in turn, swiftly drove a knife into the Joker's head. Like I said, off the rails fast! Darline thought about shooting the injured man, but the chaos around her dictated she leave immediately. She wasn't happy about leaving the job half done (her words, not mine), but realized she needed to go.

Now, you need to understand something about my wife; she's not a violent person. Even killing bugs bothers her... I'm not kidding. I've had to *humanely* remove some of the biggest, nastiest hornet-wasp hybrids from our sunroom using a cup and a piece of cardboard. Then, set them free outside, because she couldn't stand the thought of killing them.

She, of course, wasn't the person tasked with corralling

the monster killer bees hell-bent on murdering any person stupid enough to get close to them. It's not good fun for me.

So, imagine my reaction after we made our first firearm purchase and the topic of actually using it in self-defense came up. I asked her if she thought she'd have a problem using it and she said, "Nope. In fact, I believe I'd be forced to kill anyone I pulled it on because they would now know we have a gun. If they got away, they might tell a friend or even come back themselves knowing what to expect." She continued, "So does that mean they come for us and kill us in our sleep? Do they subdue us and do God knows what? No, I'd kill the person; it's the only logical course of action." And… now you know why I'm afraid of my wife.

When I told her I didn't understand how she could say that and reminded her she wouldn't even kill an ant, she said, "Humans are the only animals that act with malice; wild animals act on instinct. That makes humans far more dangerous and more likely to inflict unnecessary pain and suffering. Not to mention committing degrading crimes against their victims."

"Holy shit," was the first thing she said when she got home. "It's happening. Your zombie apocalypse is really happening."

I'm not sure how I became the owner of said apocalypse, but I didn't interrupt.

"Are the guns loaded and placed around the house? Are all the magazines loaded and within reach of the corresponding gun? Are the ready bags ready?"

I started to answer after each question, but the next question came so rapidly I only had time to nod my head. Finally I blurted out, "Yes to all of that, I've also gassed up the generator and worked on fortifying the fence. I was waiting until you got home to work on the gate. It's a weak spot but using the Jeep to block it should work for now."

At this point, we believed it wouldn't last past a few weeks. It was unfathomable that we would fall... we're RAM, we always come out on top. If we survived the Split, we should be able to survive anything.

We didn't realize exactly how bad things had gotten. BSU was already descending into absolute bedlam. The reduced military and police presence, plus an unarmed civilian population, allowed the unrestricted spread of the virus. They were already on the verge of collapsing.

As we walked around the house checking on our readiness, I noticed her looking at my midsection with a curious expression on her face. Before I could speak, she asked, "Why are you so bulky-looking?"

Now, I had planned on telling her why, but something happened when she asked the question. My mind immediately clicked into self-preservation mode and I said, "I told you I gained weight this year. Looks like you just now noticed." And recklessly added, "It hurts that you don't listen when I talk."

With an eye-roll and ever so slight hint of frustration in her voice, she asked again, "Why are you so bulky and box-like in your chest and midsection?" You'll notice the additions to her original question. She was signaling that she realized I was hiding something.

My response was that of any man in my position. "What?" I said, with a shrug of my shoulders and my best *I do not understand what you're talking about* look on my face.

Realizing she was getting nowhere fast, she smacked me in the chest and exclaimed, "I knew it, you've got your Kevlar vest on. You understand that these things don't have very good motor skills, and that civilization hasn't descended into chaos yet, don't you? And those gangs of crazed killers that I'm sure in your mind are already rioting in the streets. They haven't even started to form in whatever dark corner you imagine them in." It gets better. "And that we own enough guns and ammunition to repel a small army from our front yard, right? You get that; please tell me you get that."

I stood, mouth agape, still trying to think of an answer to her first question when she launched another salvo at me.

"And you better get my vest ready for me. Or the crazy people I'm now forced to think about because you planted the seed in my brain will be the last thing you should worry about." She finished up with a classic stink eye.

I felt a little smacked around after the one-sided exchange. So I simply turned around and headed upstairs to our bedroom and pulled out her vest. Of course I had hers ready, I was waiting for the right time to tell her. And to tell her we needed to begin wearing them full time. With everything going on, I simply forgot. And, like most men, I felt like she busted me doing something wrong… it's all in the tone our wives use, right? It's all in the tone!

After we got all of that taken care of, and I had shaken off the verbal assault, we started contacting friends and family. It was shocking how little they knew about the virus. How could you not know? For the love of sweet baby Jesus, you should have heard something by now. Even by accident. I directed them to turn on the news and call back after they figured it out.

I have two brothers. One of them, Stone, and I have talked about things like this for years. And even though we never considered zombies as a possibility, we figured something would "blow up" and we should be prepared. That morphed into buying supplies at gun shows, hence the police surplus Kevlar vests, or finding something online that would work *just-in-case*. It was fun, at the time. Now we're the smartest guys in the room.

To be clear, we do not have rooms full of supplies, but we are ready for a relatively long period of unrest. Darline expressed a little surprise at how ready we were. She knew I bought "stuff" but didn't pay close attention to it. She figured if it kept me occupied, it, in turn, kept me out of her hair. We often talked about the weapons and ammo, but not the food and other supplies. Once, she asked me what would happen when we ran low on food. I explained, with a wink, that's when we load the guns and go shopping.

So, back to my brother, Stone. We planned to hole up in our homes if possible and consolidate, if needed, to the more secure of the two. If both got breached, we had two rally points where we would meet up and caravan to our eldest brother Jack's home.

Jack lived a little off the beaten path with land around him and a small population of neighbors. We didn't actually clear this plan with him. But it was only a *what if* plan, something we talked about while having coffee after shooting on weekends.

CHAPTER 7:
THE FIRST NIGHT

The first night remained quiet until 2:30 a.m. Not able to sleep, I kept looking for fresh news about the outbreak. The only thing we knew for sure, at this point, was that it spread incredibly fast.

A scream shattered the quiet. It came from behind our house. I ran to the bedroom window which faced the backyard and our neighbor's house. Several sections of the street were visible between the homes. The streetlights provided enough light that seeing wasn't an issue as long as the houses or landscaping didn't block my view.

I saw nothing for a long minute. Then suddenly she ran into view, covered in blood and screaming at the top of her lungs. She used a rag to staunch the blood flowing from a wound on her neck. The amount of blood loss shocked me as it streamed down her body, staining her white shirt a deep crimson.

I opened the window to tell her that I was coming to help. But as I opened my mouth, she was dragged down by a man covered in even more gore than her. She obviously knew him because she kept asking him why, and the question always started with the name Kevin. I yelled to Darline to call the police and lined up my shot. I recognized what was happening, and that I needed to stop it from spreading.

When Kevin came into view through my scope, I couldn't believe what I saw. The tattered mess named Kevin was hemorrhaging through strips of skin hanging from his face and arms. He literally looked like someone had cut him to ribbons.

The cuts on his arms ran so deep that bone glinted in the light cast by the streetlamps. Adjusting my scope, I lined up the woman and saw a large, gore-covered hunting knife in her hand. I realized the cuts on Kevin came from the brutal defense the woman had mounted. She brought the knife up to defend herself once more while Kevin attacked her on the street, but her arm fell harmlessly to her side.

Testing the theory that body shots are useless, I shot Kevin in the chest. Other than knocking him off of the now motionless woman, it had little effect. He wobbled around as he tried to get to his feet and presented his head to my scope's crosshairs. I took the shot and watched his head snap back with his body following soon after. The shot ended him and his attack.

The realization that I had shot another human began to set in when the woman began to stir.

My first thought was, *She's not dead, she's trying to get away.* I was wrong. She was getting to her feet but not to escape; she had turned. I realized this after seeing the severity of the wound to her neck. There was no chance she'd lived through that amount of trauma. The ragged, gaping wound exposed part of her trachea and jawbone. An extraordinary amount of blood poured down her shirt and pooled at her feet. She stood on unsteady legs and seemed to look in my direction, but with no focus. I knew what I had to do, and I did it.

Darline walked into the room after the second headshot. She looked confused by the shots and, moreover, by what I was shooting.

The stunned look on my face didn't clear up her confusion. We stood staring at each other while reality sank in; it was already in our neighborhood. The virus was one street over and would reach our doorstep soon.

Darline finally said, "911 is busy, I tried them four or five times and it's busy."

"Well," I said, "nothing they can do for Kevin or his girlfriend now."

Darline looked puzzled, then the pieces fit together as she glanced out the window. "No, I don't think they can help them. It's just going to be you and me against this thing, isn't it?"

"That's what it looks like; that is indeed what it looks like," I responded.

A crash against our fence drew our attention. It shuddered violently as something attempted to bust through. I bolted downstairs and into the backyard to investigate, telling Darline to cover me from the window.

The small amount of fortifying I'd completed appeared to help the fence withstand the assault. It also made me feel like a genius for thinking to do it!

When I arrived in the backyard, I realized I didn't have a plan. If the fence failed, I was in trouble. The thought didn't help me put a plan in place, but it motivated me to take cover and start working on one.

Since our garage backed up to the fence, with about two feet between them, I decided climbing on the roof was my best option. I grabbed the ladder from inside the garage and set about getting to the roof.

The monsters on the opposite side of the fence both saddened and terrified me; they had been the Johnson twins. They lived across the street from our backyard neighbors. Rumor had it they were nice kids. Though I couldn't recall their names, I guessed them to be about sixteen years old and both looked like athletes.

They still wore their baseball uniforms, indicating they'd just come from a game or possibly practice. Their arms were covered with bite marks, and one of them was missing an ear. Their eyes were the color of spoiled whole milk.

The twins worked diligently trying to destroy our fence, and I couldn't allow that to happen. I brought my Ruger AR to my shoulder and placed the crosshairs on the first Johnson boy's head and stroked the trigger. He hit the ground before I recovered from the recoil. His brother became agitated and increased his assault on the fence until he met the same fate.

I wasn't okay with taking these kids' lives and had to remind myself that they were no longer kids. They had become killing and eating machines.

Sirens screamed in the distance, growing to a fevered pitch. Eventually, it sounded as if the entire city emergency services fleet had been activated.

I made my way off the roof and into the garage to get some wood and the leftover vinyl fencing slats. The windows on the lower level of the house needed to be covered immediately. I thought we would have more time before we needed to worry about it. Boy, was I wrong.

We have seven ground-floor windows, with one being glass block and two facing the backyard. I worked on the front windows first and planned to have every window covered by daybreak.

The sounds of gunfire and sirens ruled the night. Darline stood watch while I covered the windows. Our street was quiet, with lights on in most of the surrounding homes. Some of my neighbors took note of our actions and began duplicating our efforts.

After working through the night, several of us held an impromptu meeting in the street. With dawn breaking and it being early summer, the morning was perfect for this kind of meeting. Well, the weather was perfect; the day wasn't. In fact, it was far from perfect.

Though most of my neighbors owned at least one firearm, I figured, other than my friend Randy, none owned as many as me. It struck me as funny how one day I'm the "crazy gun nut" but today I'm suddenly an asset.

The meeting lasted about twenty minutes. We decided to take turns watching our street from elevated positions on rooftops and trees—anyplace offering the height needed for a clear and expanded view of our surroundings. But, more importantly, we needed to convince our neighbors to take an active role in our security.

We decided that we would split into groups of two and pay a visit to every house on our street. Inform our neighbors of our plan, press them into service, and ask them to come to a block meeting.

More significantly, we needed to ensure no infected persons were in any of the houses. If you just asked yourself, *How the hell are you going to do that?* you asked the same question we did.

Nevertheless, it needed to be done. But not one of us had military training, nor had we ever cleared a house of anything more than an ant infestation. Talking our way into a house, clearing it and possibly killing a loved one of the person who let us in was something altogether horrifying.

Patricia, from across the street, was in her early seventies and tough as nails; you'd never guess her age. She stood straight as an arrow with clear, intelligent eyes. Only her graying hair, pulled into a tight bun, betrayed her age. Oh, and if she heard me call her Patricia, she would most assuredly throat punch me.

She recommended calling each house first and asking

some neighborly questions: *Is anyone in the house sick? Are you aware of what's going on in the world?* It was a solid plan and should be faster and safer to execute.

Pat directed us to gather up our neighbors' numbers and get on the phone. She still had a landline, which we all did, and it was working fine. But cell service kept returning an "all circuits busy" message.

Ellen Anders, Will Noting, Andy Wilms, and Barb Falling all headed home to start the task... I did not. Pat looked at me and asked if I needed something. I replied in the negative. With a look of understanding crossing her face, she said, "You don't have any phone numbers, do you?"

I tried to correct that assumption, but it was a little feeble when I said, "Not true, I can call Allen Day on the corner, and Randy."

Pat shook her head and said, "You do that. And when you finish, maybe go door to door and introduce yourself to your neighbors. Seeing you've lived in this neighborhood for seventeen years, and you don't know them, now may be a good time to introduce yourself."

I'm really not a social person, not a jerk, but not social with the people in my neighborhood. Well, possibly a bit of a jerk. I believed in the "good fences make good neighbors" philosophy and it worked for me. I never had to lend a tool to anyone, and that means I never had to chase any of my tools down.

Anyway, after Pat finished, I decided that I wasn't about

to start the door to door until after they finished making the calls.

I called Al. He was okay, but his son, Dillan, hadn't made it home from work and should have been home an hour ago. From what Al was seeing on the news, the route Dillan normally used to drive to and from work looked like a violent mess.

He worked across the freeway from the airport at the CSX Switching Station. I almost told Al not to worry, but he knew better, and it would have insulted his intelligence. Al and I are good friends, so I told him the truth, "It's going to be a long, hard-fought return home, Al. And make sure you check him for bites and scratches before you let him in." After a long silence, I followed up with, "If you can't do it, call me and I'll come down and do it for you."

Al understood the double meaning in my statement and we hung up with the agreement that he would call if he had to.

The call to Randy was easy. He seriously answered the phone by saying, "I haven't been bitten, and my wife's accounted for."

I figured that would be the case and told him I would be in touch soon. Well, I made my calls. Time to wait out the others. See, it doesn't pay to have a lot of friends, it turns into work. One way or another it turns into a lot of work!

CHAPTER 8:
CALLS HAVE BEEN MADE

They completed the calls in under an hour and most of our neighbors understood why they were called. We had two houses on our street in question, and several more still waiting on loved ones to return home.

The results were better than I'd expected. The group started making calls to more homes in the development, not just people on our street, and other than the monsters I killed earlier, things seemed okay.

As for our street, we needed to check the two houses. Those houses belonged to Tesha Finnie, who should have been home because she works nights, and Westley Newcomb. I like Tesha. The ten words we've exchanged over the years had always been pleasant. Westley, on the other hand, always looked constipated and searching for a fight to help release that pent-up *pressure*.

We met in the street again, joined by other neighbors that we pressed into service. All carried at least one firearm, and most carried more than two. We decided to check on Tesha and her five-year-old son first. Tesha was someone that as of yesterday I wouldn't have worried about. She seemed tough. And I assumed being a single mom who had lost her husband to the war in Afghanistan made her that much tougher.

However, yesterday was gone; today people you loved and trusted could turn into monsters and kill you or literally eat you alive. Not in the *my in-laws are killing me* or the *my wife is eating my soul* kind of killing and eating. The real, sinking of teeth into your flesh and eating you. The kind that kills you.

I stopped, press-checked my CZ P07, and headed to Tesha's house with a small group of volunteers. We spread out, one at the front door, one at the back door, and one on the left side with direct lines of sight to the front and back doors. With more people positioned along the perimeter of the yard, we would be able to contain anything trying to *squeeze* out of the house.

I assigned myself the front door. I'm not sure why, I don't move as fast as I once did and would surely be bowled over and eaten whole before my brain chose a direction for me to run. But I did it anyway. I was hoping that when I opened the door, we'd find nothing at all. No monsters, no blood-soaked walls and floors, and definitely no bodies or body parts for that matter. Just a house frozen in time.

So, I geared up, took deep breaths, cracked my neck like a prizefighter, braced myself and… well, I knocked on the door. I didn't see a reason to kick it in. Not that I could kick it in. I'm getting old, not soft, mind you, I still work out, so I'll go with older. Also I'm not a carpenter and didn't want to replace the door if nothing was wrong in the house. So, I knocked and yelled for Tesha. There was no response, so I knocked again. Still nothing. I tried the door to see if it was unlocked. It was. I looked back at Randy and he gave me a *go ahead* nod so I pushed the door open.

I immediately found myself staring directly into the muzzle of the single largest handgun I had ever seen. The bore seemed as big as a half dollar, partly because it was level with my eyes and about a half centimeter from the bridge of my nose.

I think I momentarily blacked out, because the next thing I heard was Tesha yelling at Randy and Will, who were both yelling at her not to shoot me. I tried to ask her the same thing, to please not kill me, but I was only able to gasp like a fish and stare at the gun in my face.

She finally looked back at me and said, "What in the hell are you doing? You almost got yourself killed. And why are you coming into my house like some kind of stalker?"

At this point, I pulled myself together enough to speak. I told her what was happening, and that we'd tried to call her. She explained that her son was sick, and she'd stayed home with him. She'd turned her phone off, trying to get some much-needed sleep.

I asked, cautiously, what *sick* meant.

"Pinkeye, you nosey stalker. Why?"

I again explained the situation, adding the information about how the virus was spread.

The look on her face told me she understood.

I only had two thoughts. *What kind of gun is she pointing*

at me? And *I don't want to catch pinkeye.* In a feeble attempt to break the tension, I blurted out the question about the gun while I backed away from the pinkeye zone.

"It's a Smith and Wesson 500 Magnum. Why, are you going to steal it from me, creepy stalker guy?"

I honestly didn't have an answer for that, so I left the pinkeye zone, thrilled to be alive and hopefully, pinkeye free! She yelled after me that if we woke up her son, she would come knocking on our doors to drop him off. She added, "Thanks for checking on us."

After calming down, we headed off to find Westley Newcomb. As we walked to his house, we noticed the gunfire in the distance had intensified. It was hitting the fan all over the city. We needed to get organized.

We took up the same formation as we had at Tesha's. This time, however, I brought my gun to the low ready position. I performed the same gyrations as before. I wanted to avoid any bullets that might exit the door, so I moved to the side. Don't ask me why, but I had a bad feeling about this guy. Like he would shoot me for fun and use the excuse that my knocking startled him.

After I knocked, nothing happened. I called out to Westley. Still nothing. I knocked again and received a thump against the door in reply. The door didn't move all that much, but enough for me to pull my gun to the high ready position. When the others saw my reaction, it sent a wave of anxiety through them. None of us are trained first responders. The thought of being forced to kill a neighbor had us breaking out in a hard sweat.

I knocked, with my foot this time, again moving to the side immediately. Again I received a thump in response. Because I used my foot, I looked down to ensure I made contact and didn't trip. That's when I noticed the blood seeping from beneath the door, the amount increasing with each thump. The thick red liquid sent me into a panic. Someone was hurt and hurt badly. I called out to Randy for help. We needed to get into this house, and we needed to do it now.

Together we hit the door with our shoulders. It was unlocked, but it only opened a few inches. We should have kept the door shut and never witnessed what awaited us. It became clear that a body was blocking the door, when, through the small opening we created, a hand splashed down into the blood. We pushed much harder at the sight of the hand, creating enough space for a body to squeeze through.

I entered first. As I squeezed past the door, I began gagging from the stench that greeted me. Then I saw it. The thumping was coming from Westley's wife's body (sorry; I don't recall her name).

Every time Westley took a bite from the remnants of her upper body, it moved back and forth against the door. Only bones and gnawed tendons remained below her waist... and so much blood, so much blood.

After dragging my eyes off of the wife, what used to be Westley came into full focus. He was covered in gore with bits and pieces of his wife stuck to his face. He had been eating in an upward direction towards her head, leaving her lower body in tatters. They were both dressed for bed, so this had been going on for at least several hours, possibly all night.

He didn't stop his feast when I entered. I yelled to Randy to stay behind and cover the door in case this went south. We needed to contain it as quickly as possible, and we couldn't let Westley get past us.

When I yelled, I got Westley's attention. He looked up from his feast, and, clearly decided I looked like a better meal than the one he was enjoying. He tried to stand, but only got to all fours before the mix of the bloody floor and diminished motor skills caused his arms to slide from under him.

I was frozen by the horrific scene. Then his bulk smacked to the floor, splashing blood all over me and shocking me back to reality. I pointed my CZ at him and ended the grotesque moment.

The gunfire brought Randy through the door like a bulldozer, sliding a foot or two past me on the blood-slicked floor. With his arms whirling and his legs scrambling for purchase, he looked like a cartoon character.

When his feet found traction, he shot forward at about a hundred miles per hour, yelling for help. I reached out to help him stabilize, but it was too late—he splashed down hard on the gore-covered floor. Luckily, he hit ass first. It looked like it hurt, but he didn't end up face first in the mess and so avoided a mouth full of gore. And it would have gone in his mouth, because he was screaming like a school girl on his way down.

When he took in his surroundings, panic and disgust flashed across his face at the same instant. He scrambled to his feet, with a lot of slipping and sliding, and headed immediately to the kitchen sink and proceeded to drench himself with dish detergent and water.

When the detergent mixed with the blood from his time on the floor, he looked like a giant blue and red tie-dyed nightmare. He stood stock still, looking around and trying to take it all in.

He looked at me and said, "I'm going home to take a shower, change my clothes, and pack up every gun I own. Then we're going house to house... every house, even if we've already cleared it, to make damn sure none... not one of these things is in our neighborhood." Randy looked me in the eyes for a ten-count and repeated quietly, "Not one of them. Are we together on that?"

I responded with a stiff nod and Randy walked out of the house, a little green around the gills, but at least he walked this time.

CHAPTER 9:
IT'LL HAVE TO WAIT

Shocked by what they witnessed, the other members of the team left to secure their homes. I decided to search the house for any monsters that might be hiding, and for anything useful to the neighborhood.

The house held no surprises, in the "people trying to eat me" kind of surprises. But the amount of firepower stashed in the house was awe-inspiring. I thought I had the stash to end all stashes. I had nothing compared to Westley's hoard. The gems of his collection were three mil-spec M4s. I'm not sure how he came into possession of them, and that wasn't important. What was important was that I wanted one of them... finders keepers.

The stash would serve us well, and the ammo might last for the next fifteen years. I'm not kidding; he had so much ammo. While pulling the arsenal out and inventorying it, I tried my cell and by some miracle got through to Darline. I told her to bring the Jeep and work with Pat on storing everything I found. I also mentioned that I wouldn't be upset if one of the M4s found its way to our gun safe.

Al called immediately after I ended my call with Darline.

"He's trapped, my boy is trapped!"

After calming him down, I asked him to clarify.

"They have him trapped in a train car by Route 237, across from the airport."

I took about two seconds to wrap my head around what he said—the location, that Dillan was in a train car, in an area full of train cars, across from the airport, probably the hardest hit area in the city—and I only had one response: "Well, let's go get him."

Randy hit my front door the same time I did, loaded for bear. Several handguns were holstered on various parts of his body, each with four magazines and two ARs slung in an "X" across his back.

The look in his eyes told me the shower and fresh clothes hadn't changed his mind. He still wanted to go house-to-house in a scorched earth campaign.

Before he asked me to suit up, I told him it would have to wait. He looked confused, so I explained my call with Al and that I was going to help him rescue his son. Randy looked hurt, like the last kid picked for the kickball team. I had to ask, "What's wrong? You can still go house to house. Grab Tesha and Darline and whoever else wants to join you, and clear the neighborhood."

My words sent him off the rails. He started ranting about me leaving him behind and that I didn't trust him because of what happened at Westley's house and blah, blah, blah.

Trying to get a word in edgewise required an insult,

and I was just the guy for the job. I said, "Randy... you're a terrible shot." Now, if that doesn't seem like a real insult, you don't understand Randy. He has a picture of every target he's used going back almost ten years. He shoots at the range two to three times a week. After each trip, he compares the targets to older ones. He has them organized by gun, caliber, ammo manufacturer, target size, distance, day of the week, date, and several other categories.

It's a bit of an obsession for him and he's wicked sensitive and competitive. It got so bad I started pulling my shots to keep him from flying into a fit by shooting better than him. And I mean a full-fledged fit! At one point, he stopped talking to me for a month. Oh, we would still go to the range, get coffee afterwards, ride to and from the range together, but he refused to talk to me.

So my saying that to him locked his jaw shut instantly, and his face turned so red it looked almost crimson. I think I saw his hand twitch and inch closer to one of his handguns.

Before his head burst from the pressure, I said, "I didn't want to assume you'd be willing to join us and face what's sure to be an extremely dangerous situation. It wasn't my place to put that on you. But, I can see from your reaction that you want to go. I'll feel better having you with us."

He responded by asking, "Why the hell did you say that about my shooting? You know how I am about my shooting. It's a cold thing to say man, cold and hard."

Explaining my tactics didn't make things better, so

I grabbed my XDm in .45 ACP, my AR, and we headed down to Al's.

When I radioed Darline and told her what we planned to do, she wasn't thrilled, but she understood. I told her to team up with Tesha and recruit some people to go house-to-house. She would also call her friend Lisa, who talks way too much, and recruit her.

After Darline's experience yesterday and despite what all the books and movies told us, we didn't hit a ton of traffic in the form of abandoned cars. However, bodies littered the roads. I couldn't tell if the bodies belonged to the infected or non-infected. My guess was a mix of both lost these mini-battles for life.

As we neared the airport, Black Hawk helicopters zipped overhead, heading to and from the airport. Our easy ride ended as we rounded the corner from Brook Park Road onto Route 237. The road was a cluster of abandoned and wrecked cars with a narrow path through the middle. We speculated that the path was intentional and related to the helicopter traffic.

The stench of death and burning flesh overwhelmed us. I had braced myself for the smells. Like I said, I'm a zombie book connoisseur, and yes, I was using that knowledge to guide my decision-making. And it had kept me alive, so far. But burning flesh mixing with the stench of death had all of us gagging and rolling up the windows.

Cleveland's airport has one crescent-shaped terminal that's split between two levels. The upper level is ticketing, departures and security; the lower level is baggage and pickup. It's not a big airport, and it's easy to navigate in and out of. It has two ramps; one for each level and they re-connect with Route 237 on the other side.

As we exited Route 237 and entered the airport grounds, we encountered our first challenge. We had planned to use the airport access road to reach the overpass overlooking the area where Dillan was trapped. But towards the top of the passenger drop-off ramp sat a military roadblock manned by two digi-cam clad soldiers. Both were watching us, one through the scope on his M4, which was a very uncomfortable feeling.

The passenger pickup area would have been our next option. However, several cars appeared to have tried to navigate the entrance simultaneously. The outcome was predictable, and the result now blocked the entrance. The cars were riddled with bullet holes, but no dead bodies were visible. Blood stained the pavement indicating that something terrible had happened here. I was convinced the soldiers had something to do with it, but I was in no position to ask them for an explanation.

When the soldiers started to assume a defensive posture, we decided to appear friendly and keep moving. The thought of getting killed on day one and a half of the apocalypse just didn't seem, well, cool. We waved and doubled back to cut through the long-term parking lot.

Our detour made it a little harder to access the overpass, but it was our only option. The ramp to the overpass was open, but this side of the passenger drop-off area was also guarded by the military, this crew manned a Humvee with a .50 cal mounted in its turret.

As we crested the top of the overpass, the full scope of how bad things had gotten hit us full on.

Route 237 consists of four lanes and separates the airport and the train yard. A rusty ten-foot-high cyclone fence, with barbed wire strung across the top, surrounded the train yard. We figured out that the stink of burning bodies came from a still smoldering car accident on Route 237. Dozens of bodies, scattered around the burned-out cars, were scorched to their bones. It appeared they had walked directly into the burning cars and they too caught fire.

The stench of death was coming from hundreds of the dead stumbling along the train tracks; they seemed to be focused on one train car in particular.

I glanced at Al and said, "At least we don't need to guess where your boy is. They've shown us the car he's in."

Al seemed relieved by being closer to finding his son, and that we had a laser focus on the car he was trapped in.

Then it hit us. There were hundreds of them... hundreds, not the ten or twenty we thought we'd find... hundreds. When we finally shifted our gaze from the walking nightmares, we started working on a plan.

The train car sat parallel to Route 237 and to our position, affording clear lines of sight and firing angles that would limit the chance of an errant round piercing the train car (Randy had brought his .308) and killing anyone inside. But we couldn't see the north side of the car, which prohibited us from determining the amount of monsters clustered in that area.

We came up with a plan that required splitting up. One of us would hold our current position while another would take a position to the north of the train car. The third would take the center position.

The center position role was awful. That person was tasked with creating a distraction in the hopes of pulling the zombies off the train car and to their position. The downside of drawing the dead to them? Nothing but a chain link separating them from hundreds of dead which we had determined want to eat us. It was also the most critical role of the three. If executed correctly, it would enable two of us to thin the herd while the things shambled in the direction of the living meat; in turn, creating a path to safety for Dillan.

We concluded we couldn't kill them all before they reached the fence, so we counted on two things: the shooters being able to kill enough dead things to cut down on the mass, and the remaining mass not being large enough to pull down the fence giving them access to an easy meal.

Al tried to call Dillan to explain the plan to him but only got a busy signal. We'd paused for a moment, thinking about our next steps, when Dillan appeared on top of the train car. He shouted to get our attention, letting us know he was ready when we gave him an opening.

Al was moving towards the fence the instant he saw his son, subsequently launching our plan into action. By default, Al would be the decoy and didn't seem to have a problem with it as he moved like a man on fire towards the fence. Randy bolted for the northern position directly after Al, and the plan came together.

CHAPTER 10:
FISH IN A BARREL??

I was confident our plan would work and started coming to grips with shooting these things that used to be human. I lined up my first shot. A smooth trigger stroke registered with a hole in the cranium of the lead dead thing (we should find a better name for these things).

Randy began hitting the north side hard with a rapid string of shots and kills. I wasn't moving as fast as Randy, and I had a feeling he'd be keeping a tally. It's what he does. Remember what I told you about Randy and shooting.

The faces of the dead in my scope sent chills down my spine. Something terrible had happened to them. Blood covered them from head to toe, and most of them had sustained an enormous amount of physical damage.

One monster, in particular, stood out. She had been scalped and her bottom jaw was missing. Her tongue flopped around the gaping hole that remained. Her exposed skull glistened in the mid-day sun, and still she moved towards Al's position. I ended her pilgrimage with a hole under her left eye. I did her a favor when I ended her life a second time.

Ten minutes later, we had killed half of the herd with

B.D. Lutz

most of the remaining things massing at the fence. As Al ran back and forth, screaming at the top of his lungs and luring them to him, Dillan made his move. He dropped from the top of the car, causing me to lose sight of him. I hoped Randy had picked him up and would provide covering fire as he worked his way towards my position. A few seconds later, Dillan came back into view and I started clearing a path for him.

I was occupied finding targets when a clatter from behind me pulled my attention away from my scope. What I found when I looked behind me nearly stopped my heart. At least ten things shuffled up the other side of the ramp in my direction. I had been so focused on what I was doing that I'd lost my situational awareness.

Yelling obscenities, mostly at myself for being a dumbass, I wheeled around with my AR in firing position, but the first thing was already on me.

The stink coming off of him was overwhelming, making my eyes water and triggering my gag reflex. The combination of involuntary reactions delayed my response to the threat by another five seconds. If not for the fact that my AR ended up positioned between the thing and my neck, I would have been a dead man.

The collision pushed me hard to my right. I instinctively pushed against it with my AR, forcing my body further off balance and causing me to stumble towards the ground. My right hand shot out, stopping my fall and helping me regain my balance. I backpedalled, putting several feet between

71

me and the monster still scuffling in my direction.

I raised my weapon and took a hasty shot which slammed into its cheek (I heard Randy in my head mocking me for that shot). The bullet's impact spun the beast violently, causing it to crash to the pavement, pulling a trailing monster down with him. I immediately put a round in each of their heads before my bolt locked back.

As I scrambled for another magazine, I was hit from behind. The force from the blow slammed me to the pavement, pinning my hands between my gun and my body. This thing had shambled from behind our Jeep, hitting me like a blitzing linebacker.

The thing had to weigh four hundred and twenty-six pounds and smelled putrid, like rotten eggs left in the sun for five days. I may be understating how bad it actually smelled.

Fear and rage took over, dumping a butt-load of adrenaline into my system. I pushed with all of my strength against my rifle. I created enough space between my body and the road to pull my right arm out and push myself over, shaking the thing off my back. It latched onto my legs, but I was in a better position to fight back.

I grabbed my XDm while pushing its head back, trying to keep its chompers from finding my skin. I started to pull the trigger but stopped myself, thinking of the possibility of the bullet ricocheting off its skull and into my leg. I dropped the gun, immediately cursing myself because I imagined it covered in scratches. Pushing the thought away long enough to grab my knife and plunge it through his skull. It went limp while releasing its grip on my legs.

But the remaining monsters still shambled in my direction. I got motivated in a hurry and scrambled to my feet, realizing I was whooped. Yes, I said it; WHOOPED. I'm a fifty-year-old man who works out. I do not train for hand-to-hand combat... do you?!?!?

Now, the lingering hungry things, leering at me like I was a chicken club from Chick-Fil-A, started closing the gap on my position. Picking up my XDm, I lined up the lead thing and ended its march with one shot. It sounds impressive, but he was only about two feet away. The best part? It was a two-fer, meaning the bullet traveled through the first thing's skull and into its companion. This may surprise you, but a bullet doesn't always stop after hitting human tissue or bone. It can change direction and move further into the body and/or exit the body, but it doesn't stop until it runs out of energy.

The second one slammed to the ground immediately after the first thing, tripping up a third. This gave me a few seconds to catch my breath and line up the most immediate of the threats in my sights.

It also gave me a chance to take another count of the things. I realized I had lost track of one, causing a cold sweat to run down my back. I shot the closest threat and immediately turned around and peered directly into the open maw of a half-naked monster.

It didn't hesitate before lunging at my neck. Why

always the neck? Moving quickly, I brought my gun up and under its chin in time to stop it from clamping onto the aforementioned neck.

However, when it hit me, it forced me off balance and I found myself on the ground for the second time in less than three minutes. This time, the thing on top of me held me in an exceptionally dangerous position, its slavering mouth only inches from my face.

As I had mentioned, fatigue had set in. My age, lack of sleep, and extreme physical exertion were taking a toll on me. I was losing this fight. Pushing with everything I had left in my tank only kept it from latching onto my neck. I wasn't able to break its grip. As its face hung about an inch or so from its target, a particle-filled blackish slime poured from its mouth onto my face and neck.

My struggle to keep my face, and in particular my mouth, from catching the slime started eating more energy. Energy I needed to keep it from latching onto my neck. I was fading fast and starting to wonder if this was how I would die. After all my preparation for this very event, I wouldn't survive past the opening days of the apocalypse.

The notion made me angry enough for one last push. As I struggled against Stinky, he suddenly launched into the air, landing several feet away. I thought, *You are one badass old man.* But I soon found that I'm really not as badass as I thought. It was Dillan. He had grabbed the thing by its shirt and launched it into the air... so yeah, Dillan's the badass, not me.

When it landed, it knotted up with the last three of the monster gang. They crumpled to the ground in a tangled heap. Dillan took a quick glance at them, spun around and grabbed my outreached hand, pulling me to my feet.

"Thanks man, I was slipping away under his weight. I lost that fight." The implication of my statement hung in the air until Dillan moved in and hugged me, and I'm talking bear hug hugging.

When he pulled back with wet eyes, he said, "I was about to die in a train car or worse yet get eaten alive. So no, Otto, thank you. You and Randy didn't have to come with my dad, yet you did and I'm alive because of it."

As Dillan finished talking, the things that had been tangled up on the street were now on their feet and blundering directly at us. I handed Dillan my XDm. It hurt a little to do it, and Darline wouldn't have been happy. She loves the XDm, but I didn't have time to worry about that.

We squared up with the remaining things, ready to do what was needed to live. Suddenly, two of them fell to the ground after the tops of their heads disappeared in a bloody mist, and the third fell when its neck exploded. The last one staggered to a stop just before its head literally evaporated.

The sounds of the shots reached our ears a second after each of the things dropped. We turned to our left to see Randy, over one thousand yards away, waving at us while jumping up and down. I was thankful for what he did to help us, but I knew I would never hear the end of how good those shots were… and they really were good shots. Don't get me wrong, he wouldn't gloat about saving our lives; he would gloat about the shots he'd made. It promised to be a long ride home.

About twenty seconds later, Al ran up the ramp directly to his son and hugged him, unable to speak. The hug said it all.

CHAPTER 11:
TIME FOR ANSWERS

Al, Dillan, and I had already loaded up by the time Randy made it back to our position. Some of the things that Al had distracted were getting through the fence and joining up with a larger herd coming from Route 237. We had to get moving.

Tired, sore, and salty, I simply wanted to go home. This was all coming at me excessively fast. I didn't want to fight anymore; I wanted to sleep.

As we were pulling off the overpass, I glanced over and saw the soldiers in the same positions as when we arrived. So, conceivably, they had witnessed the entire fiasco playing out and hadn't taken a single action to assist.

Now, like I said, I was salty, and I got this ping of anger after seeing them. I decided to find out why in the holy hell they hadn't offered any help. I understood they didn't have any sight lines that afforded them any meaningful shots at the monsters attacking me. But they should have moved and TRIED to set up a good firing position. Maybe pulled the trigger ONE time and killed one of the THINGS trying to EAT me.

As I wheeled around to head up the ramp to ask them

why, a deafening silence fell inside the Jeep. All eyes rested directly on me. That's when I realized I had been ranting out loud, not in my head as I'd assumed. I do that from time to time, it's a bad habit that drives Darline crazy.

Randy spoke first. "Are you sure about rolling up on the guys with the fifty-cal pointed at us?" He continued, "And you're going to demand what? That they answer to you about why they didn't help the guys that purposely agitated the dead things and, unsurprisingly, got into a jam and almost got killed? Is that your plan?"

"Well, Randy, when you put it like that, it sounds like a great idea, doesn't it? The kind of idea that might get us all shot in the face." I kind of yelled when I answered him, and once again the Jeep interior fell silent as its occupants gawked at me. Apparently I was a little more worked up than I realized as I stared back at them with psycho eyes.

Dillan broke the silence when he said, "Otto, if that's your plan, I'll wait at the bottom of the ramp for you to finish talking to them." He was joking, I think.

I turned around and without missing a beat, I transformed into my father and said, "Dillan, don't *make* me come back there."

The tension snapped and we broke into uncontrollable laughter, tears streaming from our eyes. Randy's *snorting* set us off again, and we launched into round two of laughter just as a knock came on the window.

The knock didn't get our attention as much as the object doing the knocking: the business end of an M249 light machine gun. It's a bad ass weapon, and I'd always wanted to see one, but not from this angle. I almost shit myself when I realized the gun was "hot" and would end all of us in about 3.1 seconds, give or take.

"Sir, roll the window down."

I understood the direction, but I was transfixed on the barrel of the gun an inch beyond my window pointing at my face... directly at my face.

Again, I hear a detached voice saying, "Sir, roll down your window, NOW."

The volume of the "NOW" snapped us to attention, and the window came down slowly. The soldier was a large man with the facial features of a twelve-year-old. An odd combination, like a giant kid that would kill all of us if we gave him a reason, or if something startled him. And, considering what was happening, plenty of things could startle this kid.

Two additional soldiers jogged past the Jeep and opened fire on several things (we needed to get a better name for them) moving in our direction. Kneeling, they took down the entire first wave of monsters in seconds. The little big man watched the soldiers as they worked, turning back only after the gunfire had stopped.

He leaned in and looked at all of us and our weapons. The small grin forming on his face reached his eyes; it gave me a good feeling about him.

"Are you guys heading to a battle that we're not aware of?" he asked.

Reading his name patch, I responded, "Willis, we came to pull Dillan's ass out of a train-sized jam. Dillan, identify yourself." He did. After identifying myself and the others, I asked the question we all needed the answer to: "Willis, what the hell's happening?"

The smile fading from his face spoke volumes. "Otto, it's bad. Those idiots in BSU let this thing get completely out of control, and it happened fast. They ran around forming support groups. They even tried to identify a class these things belonged to so they could protect them from persecution. They got so preoccupied being 'woke' that by the time they acted, New York and L.A. were lost."

He noticed my reaction when he brought up protecting them from persecution. He nodded and said, "Yes, protecting them from persecution, can you believe that shit? It's like back before the Split when they started to label everyone as a *special class* that needed the government's protection. They were in their glory, man. They had someone to protect and they had the opportunity to create new derogatory names for anyone speaking out against the things."

He paused, checking on the abominations walking our way. The soldiers had drawn a bead on the herd, and he seemed satisfied that we had a few minutes, so he continued, "They started calling people 'Zombiphobic'... do you believe that shit? The virus was spreading unchecked for days in BSU. They lost a city a day while taking no action. Meanwhile, we were fighting it all over RAM and reinforcing the wall. Our airports became our weak spots. Flights were in the air with infected on board because some of them took longer to turn. When they landed, some planes had ninety percent infection rates. They spilled out of those planes, and, well, you know the rest."

I asked him, "So, that's the interest in Cleveland's airport?" He raised a questioning eyebrow. So I continued, "The reason the military has it sealed off, because of what was happening with the flights?"

Willis nodded and explained that Cleveland was a key location for deploying troops to the northern mid-west and its location near the railway and Great Lakes was critical.

He explained that BSU had lost O'Hare in the first two days of the outbreak, making Cleveland's airport a strategic location. The military was launching flights to beat back the zombies massing at the Entry Point Gate separating Illinois and Indiana. The helicopter traffic we'd been seeing were resupply runs for the troops on the lines.

He finished by saying something Clevelanders have always known, "So this place is important to the survival of the north coast."

The word *survival* set me off. I was back to them not doing anything to help us. Randy noticed my change in posture and tried to pull me back, but I was already talking, and I was loud. "So, survival, you say there, Willis? That's funny, because we've been trying to survive while you and your boys were hanging out."

I was in full-blown screaming mode when Randy

finally stopped my tirade by slapping me in the shoulder…
hard. When I snapped out of it I realized I really had gone
off the deep end on Willis.

Willis stared at me with his left eyebrow arched higher
than I had ever seen anyone arch a brow. I couldn't read his
overall demeanor, but he clearly wasn't pleased with me. I
didn't care because I'd just finished fighting for my life and
the lives of my friends with no help from these well-armed
men. Very well-armed, I might add.

Willis asked me if I had gotten it all off my chest. After
I nodded, he asked me, "How many rounds did you go
through while sniping those zombies?"

Willis flinched when his men opened fire on a new
batch of things that were getting too close. I started to open
my mouth, and Willis stopped me. "Not enough to take all
of those things down, that's the answer, not enough. Take
a peek at the top of the hotel. You see them?"

I bent forward and craned my neck to the right, between
the windshield and dashboard, seeing nothing, until they
both stood up to reposition themselves to support the men
covering us.

Willis picked up where he'd left off. "We had your
six the entire time. The ones that came in from your right
flank moved in under cover of the jersey barriers. By the
time we had eyes on them, they were *danger* close to you
and that big fat head of yours kept getting in the way. Next
time I'll give the okay to shoot and let things fall where
they may." Willis smiled as he finished… not a warm smile,

not hateful, but not warm.

I felt like a bit of an ass, not a complete ass because I was still pissed and needed to redeem myself. It's as crazy as it sounds. So I countered with, "My head is not fat, a little square, but NOT FAT...."

"And why's the government keeping information from us?" I asked while trying to rebound and turn the argument in my favor.

Willis, with a puzzled expression on his face, asked, "Do you have a radio in your car? Do you have a TV at home? How about a cell phone? Any of the previously mentioned items... at all, even one of them?"

I became flustered because I knew where he was going, so I did what I do when I'm losing an argument. I avoided the obvious answer, and I objected to the question as insulting, at which point Willis leaned in and turned the radio on.

The radio broadcasted a man with an authoritative voice. Willis asked me to check all the channels. I selected a dozen presets and found the same voice broadcasting on all of them. Willis explained that the grid was good for now, and RAM's broadcasting capabilities remained solid and heavily protected.

"We should be good for a while, as long as we keep the spread contained," was the message conveyed by Willis, and I liked the message.

After Willis finished talking, Randy took the opportunity to tell me to apologize to Willis. He was condescending as hell when he said it; I mean super condescending, like I was a five-year-old. Now, I already wanted to throat punch him for the shot to my shoulder and now I would have been fully justified in doing so. But I held myself in check. *This time!*

As I worked out how my attack on Randy's throat would start, shots rang out from the soldiers that had been holding the line. Willis glanced over and his expression and body language told me that bad things were happening!

He told us to move our asses as he headed towards the action bringing the M249 to life. The sound that gun made was impressive. It's actually a little sexy… you need to be a gun guy to appreciate that comment. From the sounds of the action behind us, things had started getting away from Willis and his squad.

I drove the Jeep a few feet forward to avoid the fire from the snipers on the hotel roof and I pulled to a stop, meeting the gaze of each man in our group. My question was clear, and it didn't take long to make the choice to wade into this fight.

I handed Dillan my XDm and three magazines. Randy and Al checked their weapons and did a quick inventory of the magazines they had left. We looked at each other, charged our weapons and exited the vehicle.

I told them to fall in behind me and we approached Willis, intending to signal to him our availability to help. When we came up behind the squad, I recognized our mistake. Willis didn't realize we were here, and with all the focus going down the ramp and tensions high, not to mention the constant gunfire, it's not a stretch to think one, or all of us... hopefully Randy... I'm only kind of kidding about that, could end up being shot. So we created our own firing line positioned up and to the left of Willis and his squad.

Moving into position gave us a clear view of the road and the reason the soldiers had opened fire. We realized how bad this thing was getting and how fast it was getting bad.

Something Willis said wasn't fitting. He said there had been fighting all over RAM for a *while*. I recognized things were going south, and that a lot of blood had been spilled. But I didn't recall any talk or videos of the fighting he'd mentioned. I made a note to ask him about that when this melee ended.

The throng heading our way was massive. It had to be two hundred strong. Ammo would be an issue if the fighting dragged on. I had four mags left; Randy and Al had the same. We would need to be efficient and controlled in our fire. Dillan would need to be downright methodical.

We quickly decided on a plan in which Randy, Al, and I would use three of our four magazines and keep one for the ride home. Dillan would play linebacker by falling back about fifteen yards to watch our flanks and provide cover if we needed to make a hasty retreat.

With the plan in place, we set up and started picking targets. What I saw in my scope will be with me until I take my last breath. The first monster I lined up was recently a woman. She may have just gotten out of the shower when her first life ended.

She was naked and her hair was wrapped up in a towel. Her body was savaged, and her legs were split open, making the bone between the muscles visible. Her stomach and parts of her intestines dangled through destroyed abdominal muscles. The skin above her waist hung in sheets, waving back and forth as she walked. The towel on her head was completely soaked in blood and gore. How it stayed on her head was the question that popped into my head. I know, so many other questions to ask, but that question stuck with me. Seriously, think about it. The amount of violence unleashed on her was extraordinary, and yet the towel appeared to have been recently wrapped around her head. I had seen enough and sent a round through the bridge of her nose, which, by the way, removed the towel.

Once we fell into a steady firing rhythm, Willis picked up on our presence. Initially he looked... uneasy would be a good description. However, it passed quickly as he gave us a nod of approval and turned back to the fight. I think he realized this had quickly turned into a different type of war. And in moments like this, when hundreds of these things suddenly appear, military and civilian forces would need to work together. If we didn't would bury each other in mass graves.

The bolt locked back on the second of my four magazines when Willis called a ceasefire. We'd managed to put down the threat, but it didn't feel like a victory. It was becoming more and more evident that we, with we being the world, had crossed a very thin line. A line that marked the crossover to a full-blown fight for our lives.

We stood silently looking at the massive amount of humanity destroyed during both Dillan's rescue and the assault from the herd. It was a sobering sight, one that brought many emotions to the surface, but an overwhelming sense of loss dominated. The loss of life, of security, and our future.

This was the beginning of the end.

Willis interrupted our reflection and thanked each one of us with a handshake.

"How can we contact you if needed?" Willis asked.

"We are about six miles from here, Willis." I gave him our location and my cell and landlines.

He mentioned something about a civilian supply program... I looked at him and my mouth dropped open. I started dreaming of having beautiful military grade equipment delivered to our subdivision. Randy punched me again.

We loaded up to head home, but before pulling out, I asked him about the timeline. He smiled and said, "We can talk another day."

It was quiet during the ride home, so I turned on the radio. No shit, they were broadcasting updates every ten minutes. RAM never stopped impressing me. It made me question my strategy of using zombie books as my survival guide. What else wasn't going to happen that was supposed to happen?

CHAPTER 12:
WELCOME YE HEROES

We listened to the radio for most of the ride home. The streets remained quiet, and the updates held no good news. BSU was in a spiral, but they still managed to turn it into political theater.

Like Willis had told us, the "self-righteously indignant" had come out in full force. They'd set up dozens of different support groups with a million rules on how to interact with the things.

They truly were in their glory. Only one problem: The things liked to eat them. Yep, bite their heads clean off and move on to the next chinless wonder before the first one realized what happened.

They didn't understand that zombies didn't need protection. They, on the other hand needed protection but didn't figure that out until far too late. As stories came over the radio of what was happening in Blue States United, we couldn't help ourselves and started laughing. The laughing continued until I had to shut the radio off because we couldn't take it anymore.

However, we'd managed to get some information on supply stations and safety centers, and even though the radio was still broadcasting, we wrote the information down. We didn't record it with a cell phone. Nope, we scrambled around the Jeep looking for a pen and paper to write the information down. Old guys with old, hard-to-break habits.

I don't know how it happened, but we somehow got it into our heads we would come home to a ticker tape parade. You know, people holding up babies for us to kiss as the community cheered our accomplishments. The reality was so much not those things... at all.

We pulled into the subdivision and were met by two armed guards standing about a hundred feet off the main road. It was Bill and Barb. When we pulled up, I powered down the window and nodded at Bill. As a retired Marine he kept himself in good shape, but he liked his pasta and beer, so his gut was a little pronounced. He's a good guy and seemed at ease with the knowledge that he had figured out at least three ways to kill everyone around him.

He leaned in and said, "Otto, we're glad to see you guys. By the way, Darline isn't happy with you. She tried to call you but found your phone on the charger in the kitchen. You may want to have a superb excuse worked out before you get home."

I chewed on that information for a second and remembered cell service was spotty at best. Yeah, I'm going with *phone lines had been ringing busy, so I didn't even bother taking my cell.* That should do it.

Bill must have been in my head as I formulated that

excuse because he said, "You didn't take a walkie with you either." Son of a... they were sitting right on the kitchen counter, charged and ready to go. I believed I could talk around that, but you know what, I was just in a fight. Actually several fights so, I'm going with... I. Was. In. A. Fight!

So I told Bill that very thing. He gave me a knowing smile and said, "We need to check you for bites. Hop out and report to that little tent."

He could tell by my confused look that I truly had no idea what he was asking. So he clarified: "Pat and Darline had us set up checkpoints at the entrances. We need to check everyone coming in for bites or scratches or really any open, fresh wounds. We're controlling access to the subdivision from the main roads to prevent the infection from entering. All incoming persons, resident or visitor, need to be checked. So far we haven't made any friends, and we've had two people try to punch me... not Barb, just me." He delivered that last bit of news with raised eyebrows, as if to say *I really don't understand why it's just me?*

Looking up at him, confusion winning the war in my head, I said, "Bill, how long were we gone? I mean, I thought it had only about been an hour. How'd this come together so fast?"

Bill chuckled, "Man, you really have been in a fight. You've all been gone for over four hours and we weren't just sitting around waiting for you. Some guy, I forgot his name, he lives on Deerfield works construction. He took a few people with him to his construction yard and grabbed some cyclone fencing. The plan is to fence in the entire subdivision ASAP. We have a group of twenty people working to dig the postholes."

The plan to use fencing shocked me. Actually, the entire setup and how fast it came together shocked me.

Our subdivision is relatively large, with about four or five hundred houses. The vast majority were built in the sixties, with the last street, Lynn, being built in the mid-nineties. Eighty percent of the homes are split levels that are nearly identical. It has two entry points and is shaped like a squat rectangle that gets a little wider at the northwest entry point. The rectangle is made up of an outer road with four individual streets sitting inside the rectangle. Both of the entry/exit points are located to the north and then east and west sides of the subdivision.

With as large as it is, the thought of fencing off the entire subdivision in a quick and efficient manner seemed an impossible task. Not to mention the houses along the outer ring of the development, which backed up to homes not located in our community. How would we handle it if they wanted to join us or if they were overrun? Questions for another day, I supposed, because today me and mine mattered the most. We'd learned that fences worked, and I'd be helping to build this one.

Bill interrupted my thoughts. "Are you going to give me any trouble, Otto? I'd really like to avoid another person taking a swing at me."

An evil grin went crooked on my face. I thought about busting his chops, then realized now might not be the best time considering the circumstances. I asked, "Who's going to search us?"

Bill seemed to enjoy what he said next. "Well," he started, "the women are being checked by Tesha. She really doesn't take any shit."

"Did you see her gun?" I asked, and his eyes bugged.

"That thing's giant," he said. "But she seemed like she was in a bad mood, so I didn't ask much about it. I'm not sure how she even carries it; it has to weigh almost as much as she does." Like I said before, the gun is huge!

I wasn't comfortable that Bill only told me who was checking the women. "Bill, who's checking the men?" I asked again.

His smile got a little wider as he said, "Well, that would be Vic, you know, Vic your next-door neighbor."

"Son of a bitch... are you kidding me? Tell me you're kidding me." Vic is a... well, he's a jackass. And the reason for my reaction is, he really is a jackass. He may be a little crazy... no, he is full-on crazy. He's my crazy Italian neighbor. Only stands about five feet tall and looks like a bulldog, stout and pissed off, all of the time. And he's missing a few teeth. He's a sight.

When we first moved into our home, he just stared at us whenever we were outside. He wouldn't look away, he just stared, not speaking, just staring... for days. The first time he spoke, he complained about our dog, Fred. His very first words to us were *Now I have to worry about a dog* (insert heavy Italian accent). We told him he didn't have to worry about Fred when in fact we had no idea if he should worry about him. We'd just gotten Fred the day prior and knew zilch about him. He could have been a vicious monster dog from Hell; we really didn't know.

The day after Vic said that, we let Fred out in the morning and continued about our morning routine. When we noticed how quiet he'd gotten, we went to check on him. Fred had pulled a Houdini and escaped our yard. But he hadn't gone far. He was, in fact, in Vic's backyard. Vic was having a fit and Fred was in full-blown crazy dog mode… good times.

The staring never stopped. Then the singing in full voice as he walked up and down his driveway started. Next came the yelling at no one. He walked up and down his driveway all day, watching everything and yelling at some invisible antagonist.

After about a week, we realized that he was just bat-shit crazy. He was probably the best guy for this job because he simply didn't care what anyone thought.

"Look, Bill," I started. "We're flipping whooped, and beat up, and need showers, and we're starving and…"

"You need to get checked," Bill interrupted. "No exceptions."

I understood why he thought we were trying to avoid getting checked, but I really didn't want to deal with my crazy neighbor.

I said quickly before he shut me down, "Bill, can you do the check, please?"

He chuckled but seemed to understand and agreed.

When he told Vic, I heard Vic screaming his head off in his thick Italian accent. It went something like this: "Why he no wanna have-a me check him? He afraida somting? He gets bit, or he just afraida be nack-ed? That jerk been nutting buta pain-ina my ass, since day he anda his stunad dog move in." About that time he poked his head out the tent flap and realized I was only ten feet away. He stopped talking and stormed his short, stout body out of the tent.

That Fred still bothered him five years after we'd said goodbye to him was a testament to his dislike for everything I did.

After the search, we all headed home. I had some purple bruises and felt like a gang of angry anarchists had beat me, but other than that, I was *golden*.

Bill informed us that we had fourteen infected houses, totalling twenty-two people that had been put down. We still needed to clear a few houses, but progress was steady. He radioed Pat, and Darline was with her. I could hear Darline yelling something about me being a dumbass for forgetting my radio as Pat talked over her tirade.

Pat said they needed help clearing the remaining houses. I told her Randy and I would join them after we ate and took boiling hot showers.

I had to duck when I walked through my front door, because Darline launched a shoe at my face. It would have hurt, and I already hurt so a head wound wouldn't be a good addition to my *conditions*.

A barrage of some of the foulest language you have ever heard followed the flying shoe. Yup, she was mad at me, but I was too busy bobbing and weaving the shoe and the verbal assault to explain that I. WAS. IN. A. FIGHT.

After she calmed down, I explained what had happened and what we had seen by the airport.

"This isn't going away in a few days, is it?" she asked, worry clouding her features. Like a puppy when it didn't get the treat you had been holding in front of it for the last five minutes. It was such a sad look.

"It's not. And considering what Willis, the soldier from the airport, told us, it may never go away. BSU fell apart and let this thing get completely out of control. We've got our issues too, but BSU let it escalate past the point of contain—"

She cut me off. "It's a shit storm; just say it, SHIT STORM."

"It is," I said. "BSU's incompetence forced RAM to deploy resources to the entry points and is forcing us to position forces along the entire wall, and that's a lot of wall to guard."

I paused for a second, my anger building at how badly Blue States United screwed this up. Their politicians were always bitching about something… anything. Sitting around waiting for someone else to take care of the big problems. Then having the nerve to complain about the people with balls enough to fix the problems. Well, this time the waiting around had cost thousands of lives, maybe millions.

After I calmed down and worked things out with Darline, that's code for I apologized for about thirteen minutes. I took a shower, shoved some food in my face and hit the door.

I realized that every part of my body was aching and bruised with some road rash tossed in for fun. It made me feel old and cranky, so I pushed through the door with some dramatic flair.

When I was outside, I realized, no one cared... nice welcome home that was. I'm wounded and had guns pointed at me, and fought dead things... but no worries, I'll go back to work!

CHAPTER 13:
WHAT'S IN THE BAG

Randy was waiting for me at the end of his driveway. At five feet ten, Randy isn't a tall guy, but he's not small. He's got a bit of a gut, but he's in good shape otherwise and powerfully built. He's always lifting weights and bragging about how much he can lift.

His shoulders are huge, like land an airplane on them huge. So, as he leaned up against his wife's car, with his hands clasped behind his head and his elbows out to his sides, he looked like a giant. He has a tight mop of kinky close-cropped auburn hair and a beard to match. Like a Chia Pet!

As I got closer, I noticed how ready he was for this. He had his MOLLE duffle so full it threatened to burst. Armed like we were going to war with the Russians, with two AR platform rifles and enough loaded magazines in his MOLLE vest, which matched his duffle, to hold a firing line for six or seven hours.

He'd strapped his battle-hawk to his back and several other bladed weapons were attached to various parts of his body. The battle-hawk was a beautiful weapon finished in a RAM flag motif. I could never find one like it, and he wouldn't tell me where he bought it. He's like that!

But it was the duffle that grabbed my attention. So I asked, "Whatcha got in the bag, Randy?"

He shot me a suspicious look, like I might club him over the head and take his sack full of goodies. His reaction made me even more curious. So I asked again and this time he reached for the bag and snatched it off the ground like it was stuffed with packing peanuts. I had to know what the hell was in that bag!

He was holding out on me and had something in the bag I wanted, no, I needed to see.

"Randy, what's in the bag? If we're going to clear houses and run around killing these things together, we need to be on the same page. So, what's in the bag?" I was working the whole *We're a team, man,* angle.

He didn't care about my distress. He just stood there looking at me with crazy eyes.

"Randy, what's in the bag, man, what's in the bag?"

His eyes lost *some* of their crazy, and he started to grin. "So, you really want to see what's in the bag?"

I let my frustration get the better of me and moved to grab the bag. Randy saw me coming and moved it behind him.

I was going to lose my mind any second because I needed to know the contents of that bag. Randy figured he'd toyed with me enough. He set the bag down and knelt on one knee next to it. He looked up at me and grabbed the zipper. I could tell he was getting excited to show me. He finally pulled back the zipper to reveal his treasure.

I noticed a lot of fabric, rolled into tight little tubes, and what looked like a baseball catcher's pad set. But what really got my attention was the package resembling Comp 4 (C4). As I eyed the black plastic wrapped bang maker, Randy started to pull out the other little goodies.

He started by unrolling the fabric while explaining they were cut-resistant sleeves, military grade. He had sets for our arms and legs and then he pulled out the shin guards, Rothco neoprene guards that also covered the knees.

He had sets of elbow pads and padded vests that wrapped all the way around the torso and fit over my Teflon vest. His smile had been growing with each item he removed.

He sorted everything into two piles on his driveway and pushed a pile at me and said, "Suit up, we will live through this."

His smile fading, he continued, "I will not go through what we went through at the airport ever again, brother. I was helpless when those things attacked you. That will never happen again."

I started to reply, and he held up a hand. "Just suit up; we're clearing some houses and keeping our home safe." He reached out and grabbed the front of my vest, pulling me in close, not kiss close, more like you would if you were furious with someone.

"Suit up, we're gonna kick some ass, got it?" he yelled and released me with a little shove. He turned back to the bag and zipped it shut.

We headed out to meet up with Jax and clear some houses. Jax is a solid guy. I even let him borrow some of my tools while he was remodeling his kitchen. He gave them back when he finished… exactly like it's supposed to work.

He may have worked some kind of security job, not a security guard, but private security. I don't know for sure because when I asked him he only said, *"I'm in security, not a security guard."*

I didn't probe any further, and he didn't offer anymore. He's average height with a medium build, nothing physically intimidating about him. But one day I was walking Fred around the neighborhood and I noticed him working a heavy bag in his garage. Let me say this. I know his hands were hitting the bag because the bag was moving, and I heard his hands hitting it. However, I could NOT see his hands as he pummeled the heavy bag. So, I made friends with him, and it turns out, we had a lot in common. But not enough to exchange phone numbers. It's a big commitment to exchange phone numbers and I don't run around all willy-nilly passing it out.

On our way to meet up with Jax, I asked Randy, "How did you come across the C4? It's not something you can pick up at the drugstore."

He just smiled and kept walking, so I asked him my next question, "Randy, it's one thing to have C4, but I need to understand *why* we have it with us."

He stopped hard and spun to face me. Looking directly into my eyes, he said, "If we fail in any of these houses, I'm taking the whole house out. Dead things and all are going up in flames. We have to do everything we can to stop the virus from spreading. Whatever it takes, we stop it now."

He was right. We couldn't let it get past us, we couldn't fail. But, I could think of a million different ways to stop it from getting past us and into our streets. Not one of them involved blowing anything up. My plan started with the back and front doors being covered while one or two people entered the house. I didn't plan on blowing anything up. Especially with me in it.

CHAPTER 14:
ONE TOO MANY

We hit Jax's house a few minutes later and Tesha was waiting with him in the driveway. It was good to see her without a big ass gun in between us, but I was concerned about why she'd joined us. So I asked her, "What's up Tesha? Don't you have a sick little guy at home?"

"Good to see you too, and my boy is good. My sister cleared security and is staying with him."

I knew where this was headed, and I wasn't okay with it. Her boy had lost his father in the service of our country. I would not let him become an orphan by getting his mother killed.

"Tesha, I don't…"

She spoke over me rather forcefully. "Otto, don't even think about talking me out of this. My family lives here too. I've got to do something about what's happening. I WILL be helping to keep us safe… have I been clear?"

We just stared at her, a little shell-shocked, but understanding how she felt. We nodded and said nothing.

The four of us started off to the Hicks' home. We hadn't been able to contact them or their neighbors, the Watsons. Both homes sat cold and dark.

The Hicks were a family of four with five-year-old

twins. We decided that Tesha and Jax would cover the exits while Randy and I cleared the house. We stacked up at the door and pounded on it to get anything inside moving. Nothing happened, not a sound. I reached for the doorknob and found it locked. I glanced back at Randy, and he gave a quick nod… shit was about to get real.

This breach and search differed from Westley's house. We now understood what might await us behind this door.

The fight at the airport taught us that they might be slow, but they just kept coming. If you let your guard down or made a mistake, you'd lose big parts of your body and die. Then you'd turn into one of them. The freeways were littered with dead bodies of people that had let their guard down.

Randy moved in and kicked the door with one giant foot. This time, unlike at Westley's house, the door swung in freely, but I wish it hadn't. I wished it was a Sunday afternoon from before now. Like any Sunday in October, when the only thing I'd be doing was watching football, debating what meat to BBQ, and which beer to wash it down with, that's what I was wishing for.

But nope, the door opened and what greeted us will never leave me and will turn my dreams into nightmares. It took about three seconds to figure out we'd be forced to clear this house of monsters that *used* to be the Hicks family. Probably pieces/parts of them, too.

The living room walls were covered in all manner

of bodily fluids and appeared as though someone tried crawling up them to get away from *something*. They'd tried so hard that they'd dug grooves into the drywall. From one of those grooves hung a finger that had been ripped from its owner's hand.

A streak of what I can only describe as oily, gooey post-humanity slime seeped across the floor, following the path of the streaked blood on the walls.

I looked over at Randy and noticed he had gone ghost-white. I almost called him Casper, but then I realized why. The finger was too small to belong to an adult. We recognized what that meant. This was turning to shit, fast!

I hand signaled to Randy that I would follow the gooey streak and he needed to have my back. I spoke that last part. We're not in the military and that's a whole-lotta words to communicate with hand signals.

I started toward the streak and Randy hung back by about five steps, his head on a swivel as he fell in behind me.

Our approach was cut short when Mr. Hicks rounded the corner from the kitchen to the living room, which was our current position.

His bottom lip and the skin below his mouth to his neck were missing. His glistening jawbone and exposed teeth gave him the look of a demented circus clown. Blood soaked his face and shirt and his hair was slick with gelatinous goo. It was like staring into the mug of Hollywood's scariest movie clown come to life!

He was chewing on something that resembled a tiny hand. I didn't have time to determine what he was gnawing on. Because as soon as he realized he had a new meal standing in front of him, he lunged at me.

I had my AR in the low ready position but didn't move fast enough to bring it up to fire. Mr. Hicks hit me in a flash and pinned my AR against my torso while pushing me back on my heels.

Before I knew it, I was falling. As I flashed back to what had just happened at the airport, Randy brushed past me. At first, I was peeved that he didn't at least attempt to break my fall. Then he plunged one of his knives into the side of Mr. Hicks' head and wiggled it back and forth. Mr. Hicks dropped hard to the floor as Randy pulled his knife free with a wet *slurp*.

I started to thank him when he lunged at me, hitting me hard and driving my back through the drywall. My AR slammed into my torso, once again trapping it between my body and another person trying to crush me.

I quickly realized that clearing houses would call for a handgun, bladed-edge weapon, or bludgeoning instrument, or all three. I started to ask him what the holy hell was wrong, but my unspoken question was quickly answered. One of the little Hicks children had hit Randy at a full run. The little bastard clipped Randy at the knees, buckling them. He threw himself forward to keep from falling backwards and in the process pinned me against the wall.

Bouncing off of me, he lurched to the right and hit the floor hard. He kicked his legs like a wild man trying to shake the little Hicks off or at least stop it from biting a chunk of flesh from his leg.

As he fell, he spun me to the left and away from him. I went to one knee and was thankful for Randy's knee pads and I'm sure he was too. That's because the little Hicks was trying to gnaw through the neoprene but couldn't get its tiny teeth through the tough material.

Even as Randy kicked his legs, the little Hicks held on like a leech, working his jaw to get to the meat under the padding.

While pivoting in Randy's direction, I grabbed my big ass Buck knife and ended the little Hicks' assault. When it stopped moving, we noticed the horrific damage inflicted on its little belly. Something had chewed through to his spine. What we assumed to be the remnants from his intestines dangled out, leaking a chunky black liquid onto the floor.

Its cherubic face reminded me that not a single person was safe from the virus. Not a single person would go untouched in this nightmare. And I would revisit all of the things I was forced to do in my sleep forever. It was the only time in my life I'd hoped to die young.

I turned to Randy and nodded at Mr. Hicks. Upon inspecting the surrounding area, we realized that we would not be looking for the second Hicks child. That's because the child's remains were scattered over the floor and hung from Mr. Hicks' mouth. We confirmed that a hand was wedged in his mouth and would be there forever because I sure as hell wasn't pulling it out.

Now we only needed to find Mrs. Hicks. After we found her and killed her we could go to the Watsons' house. But a bloodcurdling scream from the front yard stopped us cold. It was a scream that carried sadness so deep it tears at your soul and promises to crush your heart.

Randy looked at me and we bolted for the front door. Once outside, we stopped hard. A woman knelt in the front yard being both comforted and restrained by Tesha.

We approached, and even though I knew the answer, I asked anyway. "Tesha, is this Mrs. Hicks?"

It was hard to hear her reply over the woman's sobs, so she nodded her confirmation.

I found no words for this poor woman who literally just lost her entire life. I kneeled down to eye level and grasped her hand. She pulled it away like I'd jabbed it with a hot poker and locked me in a withering stare.

Fury filled her features and through gritted teeth she hissed at me, "Don't touch me, you son of a bitch."

I was taken aback at first, but I understood that my presence was only making it worse.

I started to remove myself, but she had more to say. "You just killed me! You killed my babies and my husband and my SOUL." She screeched the words at me with such hatred it caused me to flinch.

She was visibly shaking, her eyes going in and out of

focus. She was going into shock and we needed to stop that from happening.

Tesha told me to leave and started working to prevent Mrs. Hicks from slipping away.

As Randy and I walked away, Jax started to follow us but I asked him to stay behind and keep an eye on Tesha.

I said, "With her focus on Mrs. Hicks, she'll be a sitting duck if one of those things finds its way in." Jax paused but nodded in agreement and took up a position a few yards away from Tesha.

I asked, "So, how much C4 do you have Randy? I think we should just blow the next one up."

He chuckled and shrugged the comment off. But I wasn't sure I was joking.

By the time we arrived at the Watson house, another team had already arrived to clear it. I couldn't have been happier to see Will leading a team of five volunteers.

Will was tall and slender with long lean muscles and a high and tight. He looked to be ex-military, but I'd never met him, and he could have been a wannabe for all I knew. However, his team was organized, stacked up, and ready to rock, leading me to believe he had at least some military training.

I was running on fumes and had a bad feeling the next several days would be much too similar to this one. But I called out to him anyway, asking if he needed one or two more bodies.

He put his team on hold and joined Randy and me. He

smiled while looking us over. "You two look like you've been riding hard. And from the sounds coming from Mrs. Hicks, things tilted sideways on you."

He glanced in Mrs. Hicks' direction as he spoke, "No, I believe you two may be one too many. Get home and get some rest. It looks like this nightmare isn't going away."

By the way, I was correct; the days that followed were pretty much identical. The end of the world was exhausting.

CHAPTER 15:
NOT HEALING ALL WOUNDS

About three weeks into this mess we had things in our subdivision relatively locked down. We were still getting probed and had the occasional breach, but we managed to keep damage and injuries to a minimum and suffered no new infections.

I contacted my brothers; both were safe and healthy. Stone set up something similar to our community but it was suffering from some infighting. He expressed concern about the long-term viability of his community. It only takes one asshole to screw everything up!

An ad hoc leadership structure started falling into place in our community. One that not everyone seemed happy with. I think it was because I somehow ended up in that structure. I'm convinced that it happened because most of the people hadn't yet met me. Apparently I come across as a nice guy... funny stuff!

Even with our controls in place, it could still be dicey to travel outside your home alone and unarmed. And despite the border wall holding back the hordes of dead from BSU, travel outside our fence remained surprisingly dangerous.

The speed with which the virus spread caused us to

have a larger than anticipated population of things roaming our streets. According to the government broadcasts, BSU was all but gone.

We realized that despite our ready bags and food from the cleared or abandoned homes, our food would run out in a few months, at best. The rule became this: The food you have in your house is yours to consume as you saw fit. Any food being held as a community basket would be rationed out in case of another disaster or an influx of survivors. All of us were to donate five cans or boxes of food. The turnout was fantastic and yielded an impressive amount of community food. An excellent start, but not a long-term solution.

The time of year would allow many of us to add to our gardens. Nevertheless, we realized it wouldn't help until harvest time. Some people tilled up their front yards and planted corn, tomatoes, and other various fruits and vegetables. But it would be a herculean feat getting adequate amounts planted in time to make a difference.

The obvious issue: We needed food, not urgently, but definitely for the months to come.

We decided to avoid the military supply centers for now. All those people crowded together, waiting for food and water seemed like a recipe for disaster. The broadcasts claimed that the supply center operations were running smoothly. Although we didn't see how that was sustainable; they would eventually implode.

Water and power were holding for now; we'd had

several outages, but nothing to complain about. A couple of our residents were electricians and, using the ample number of generators and solar panels in our community, started working on a bypass system.

Interruption of the water supply would be a different issue altogether. We were not gravity fed and getting the pumps back online would be out of scope for us. The city had a water tower that would hold us for a while, but depending on demand, it might deplete quickly.

RAM deployed the National Guard along with regular Army troops to ensure the power grid remained functional and potable water supplies remained constant. But we knew the supply of both would eventually be cut off.

We called an impromptu meeting of the entire community. At a couple hundred strong it took a bit of doing to get us all together. We talked to everyone about the food, power, and water, and decided we needed to start supply runs, especially for food and bottled water. Only if things went south would we visit the military supply stations.

I volunteered for one of the scavenger teams. Darline wasn't happy about that, but we needed food and I wasn't going to ask others to get it for me. We ended up with more volunteers than we had counted on!

During the meeting, someone asked what might happen if they wanted to leave and join one of the military safe zones. The question caught us off guard because this wasn't a police state and we wouldn't stop anyone from leaving. Re-entry might be an issue if you came back sick or worse. But leaving wasn't a problem.

However, considering the implications, we figured we needed to put some rules together. We let them know they were all free to go and would be welcomed back if they returned. Property left behind would be secured for thirty days. After thirty days, abandoned property would be forfeited to the community.

All we asked was that they advised us they were leaving. Doing so would let us secure their house and property and keep track of our population.

Seventy-five people decided to try the safe zones, bringing our population to just over one hundred. The reduction took its toll on getting the fence fully secured. We needed to get creative with scheduling for the safety patrols we were running, but we got it done. So far, the apocalypse wasn't living up to my expectations.

CHAPTER 16:
SUPPLY RUN NUMBER 1

We met in the street the morning after the community meeting. Our street meeting was comprised of the same group as before, mostly. Pat, Will, and Andy were there. Barb Falling had opted for a safe zone. Randy joined us. As always, he came loaded for bear. We were literally all loaded for bears of varying sizes!

"Well, here we are, still breathing." Pat opened the conversation; a slight but sad smile creasing her face as she spoke. "When we talked last night about organizing supply runs, we had more people to worry about getting through the next few months. We don't have as many mouths to feed now. We could push scavenging off a few more weeks."

I responded to her by pointing out, "You don't sound like you believe we can wait, and I don't think we can either." I looked around at the other volunteers. "We need to figure out how bad it is. Hit some stores to see what's left and scan the area for pockets of survivors. Maybe talk to them about initiating supply trade."

With that, we settled it, grabbed two pickups, and headed for the main gate. We'd said our goodbyes, but people still came to see us off.

Dillan was working the main gate as he did most days. He stopped us on the way out and, again offered to join us.

"Dillan, thanks for the offer, but we really need you at the gate. If we have any problems and the main gate falls, this whole place could be overrun in a matter of minutes."

It looked like his chest puffed up with a little pride when I said that. He responded with a stiff nod and finished opening the gate.

To this point we had only ventured outside the fence a few times to clear away bodies that blocked the gate. It was still wicked dangerous, but the area immediately around our subdivision was in decent shape. Only a few houses appeared to be complete losses in terms of being damaged or burned. Why are there always fires? It was just like in the books, houses just start spontaneously combusting. Like people run around inside them with oil lamps looking for a reason to drop a lamp and create even more craziness in the world!

We made a note to figure out how our community would deal with a fire if one were to break out. I think we all saw the hydrants and assumed the fire department would respond. That's how it worked, when we still had a fire department, but we weren't sure we still did. And the world was ending, soooo we ought to figure that out.

Aside from the damaged and burned homes, a lot of them looked empty. I speculated that their occupants had either fallen back to a secondary location or joined one of the safe zones.

We attributed the relative calm in the area, and the abundance of twice dead bodies scattered about, to the guards we had posted and patrolling our area. We also had guards on elevated platforms, allowing them to extend their view and ability to identify threats and neutralize them. The plethora of dead bodies made us realize we would need to form cleanup crews... should be fun getting volunteers for that job.

We opted to check one of the two drugstores on opposing corners of an intersection about a mile and a half south on the main road. With the building's windows positioned high in the walls, it would offer better protection as we scavenged. Randy and Will led the way in their truck while Andy and I followed at a safe distance.

None of us anticipated anything of value would be left behind, especially in a drugstore. The lure of all that medication, sitting unguarded, would prove too tempting for some to ignore. Not to mention people that needed certain medications to live would have undoubtedly found a way into this building.

We decided that if the store had medications left behind, we would clear the shelves and take it back to the community to distribute as needed. Two of us would search the pharmacy while the others filled the trucks with food and water. Randy and I would head to the pharmacy area while Will and Andy scavenged for food and water.

The front of the store had taken heavy damage. The

doors had been shattered inward and ripped from their guiderails with great force. Something told me this was going to suck.

We pulled both trucks directly in front of the building with their driver's sides facing the wrecked doors. We waited a minute in case the noise from our arrival provoked any of the things out of hiding. There were cars in the parking lot, indicating the store or surrounding area was still occupied. Alive or dead was the only question, and either could be deadly to us in this situation.

After about three minutes, Randy's voice broke over the walkie-talkie. "Okay, I've seen no movement. You cowboys ready to saddle up?" He had a curious Southern drawl when he said it, and I couldn't let it go.

"Hey, Billy The Kid, did you bring horses?" The incredibly long pause told me I either hit a nerve, or he didn't understand what I was talking about.

I was about to clear the air when my question was answered by a simple, "I might hate you."

I couldn't stop laughing and had to calm down a bit before I replied, "Naw you don't, you love me, you know you do."

I put the radio down and exited the vehicle. I kept an eye on Randy until I was sure he wouldn't try to exact a little revenge, but he let me slide this time.

We debated over leaving the keys in the trucks, but decided not letting them get stolen was the better idea. Don't get me wrong, these weren't Ford Raptors or Ram

1500s we're talking about. Nevertheless, they were our rides home, so keeping them was paramount.

If the person with the keys got killed, the keys might become unreachable—essentially the same as someone stealing our trucks—so we placed the keys in the rear passenger side wheel well of each truck. We did it while the others blocked us from view with their bodies while removing both the full and empty backpacks and duffle bags from the truck beds. Fingers were crossed that this worked out, and we didn't need to remember the location of the keys during a hasty retreat.

Because the doors were already breached, we entered the store quickly. The stench hit us immediately. If the flesh hanging from the shattered doors was an indicator, people hadn't made it out in *excellent* health.

After scanning the area and making enough noise to draw out anything shambling around the store, nothing stirred, so we advanced in the directions we had assigned ourselves.

The store had witnessed some extreme violence. A tremendous amount of blood mixed with unidentifiable bits and pieces was spread across the floor.

Our shoes tracked through tacky, drying gore, slowing our advance to a virtual crawl. The path of violence was easily followed, and it ran in the same direction we needed to travel. Dozens of people must have been caught in the slaughter because hundreds of bloody footprints inundated the floor.

A bead of sweat ran down my forehead as my anxiety began to build. We'd geared up much like Randy and I had when clearing the Hicks' home, and it was adding to my production of perspiration. I held my XDm so tight that my hands hurt and my forearms started cramping. My grip might prove dangerous in a burst of action, so I concentrated on relaxing my hands in hopes the cramping would lighten up.

When we found the pharmacy, it looked as I expected. Trashed! Shelves had been flipped over and the safe holding the controlled substances was badly damaged but remained sealed.

Randy and I noticed something at exactly the same time. No blood in the area. With the amount in the rest of the store, I expected this area to be a bloodbath. But, other than some bloody footprints, it was relatively free of the gore covering the rest of the store.

The stench still permeated the area. Even though the amount of blood and body bits would generate a terrible stink, it shouldn't have been this bad. It put us on edge because it meant that one or more of those things was close or we'd soon find a fully dead body.

Although the pharmacy sat in shambles, we found large amounts of medication left behind. Apparently the people raiding the area only wanted narcotics, missing the value of the other drugs.

I shook my head when I saw the shelves containing Pseudoephedrine were cleaned out. Looked like Meth hadn't lost its luster, even during the apocalypse. I didn't get it. Why would you want to be wide awake for this crap?

Randy volunteered to fill the duffels with as much medication as they would hold while I covered him from the other side of the counter.

The pharmacy housed three sets of shelves in back and two in the front, flanked by the obligatory service counter separating it from the main store. The shelves at the pharmacy's front had been flipped over, creating a small roadblock for Randy. He said he'd start with any medication ending in "cillin" and then move on from that point. Some anti-inflammatory meds were also in order.

As he put his foot on the first tumbled shelf, I turned to cover the approach to the pharmacy. Sweat spilled from my pores. This stress promised to be impossible to deal with and might turn out to be the way I died. I thought about telling Randy to grab some antidepressants when my thought was cut off by a startled yelp from Andy, followed by two gunshots. I'd known this would suck, and that suck had just started.

Randy turned, but I waved him back to keep filling the bags while yelling out, "Will, Andy, what the hell was that? You gave me a heart attack." A long pause passed with no response until someone fired another shot. "Shit, shit, shit," was all I could say as I moved in the direction of the shots. "Andy, Will, what's going on?" I asked again.

"I don't know, Otto. I've lost sight of Andy."

Will sounded panicked and in unison we yelled out for

Andy, this time getting a muffled response of, "Mmmover thisss waaaay." It sounded like Andy was talking through a pillow and struggling to get the words out.

Will and I met up at the aisle leading to the cooler where Andy should have been but wasn't. Will yelled, "Son of a bitch, he's supposed to be here. We were to keep within eyesight of each other. He should be right here."

We ran down the aisle and rounded the corner, each facing a different way to cover our flanks.

My stomach dropped when I saw the largest person... now thing... I'd ever seen. He had to weigh in at about four hundred pounds; clearly having never missed a meal in his life. He rested face down as his fat jiggled around, making him look like spoiled milk and doorknobs poured into a giant water balloon.

As I prepared to put an end to Mr. Jiggles, I noticed four feet. Two facing toes up and two facing toes down. It hit me. We'd just found Andy and Mr. Jiggles was going to crush him to death if we didn't act quickly.

I called Will over to help free Andy from under Mr. Jiggles' girth. We traded our guns for knives and cautiously approached the tangled pair. Andy struggled just to breathe because Mr. Jiggles covered all of him with only his nose and eyes showing in the crook of Jiggles' neck.

The massive thing wore a store smock. I had a feeling he'd been eating his way down the candy aisle on an average day. Then he'd switched to humans, eating the entire store staff and a few customers (the guy was huge).

122

He was covered in ichor and surrounded by chunks of his last victim. It looked like he'd just been lying there in a bloody pool, probably waiting for his next meal to come to him. Like an alligator. I swallowed hard.

We soon realized that dispatching Jiggles wouldn't be much of an issue. He was fully focused on getting to the food trapped under him and didn't notice as we approached. He struggled to get Andy into biting position, but due to his size and the way he'd landed on Andy, he wasn't able to get his mouth lined up for a bite. I slammed my knife through his skull, ending his struggle. His full girth then settled on Andy, and he was not happy about it!

We acted fast to push Jiggles off of him. Will took his lower half while I got his enormous upper body. It took all of my strength to push the fat ass off Andy. Our hands sank into his mass, causing unidentified liquids the color of sewer water and consistency of tapioca pudding to leak down our arms. I could have hugged Randy for providing the extra gear. Especially the gloves and arm pads, as they kept the skin-to-goo contact to a minimum. But they did nothing to lessen the stench coming from the goo… I almost passed out. It smelled like roadkill mixed with ammonia topped off with some actual human feces!

Will started to gag, and I didn't think he'd be able to hold back the contents of his stomach. I looked away because the goo was already overwhelming. If I saw Will vomit, I would end up joining him and we would cover Andy in even more foulness. He choked it back, and after about five minutes, we were able to move Jiggles off of Andy; more a slide than a lift.

Jiggles flopped to the side with a wet slap, freeing Andy. He got to his feet faster than I thought he would after being trapped for so long, but he had plenty of motivation. He wanted the goo off of his person, and primarily off of his face. It was so nasty, and he smelled so incredibly bad.

He had several deep scratches on his arms and one on his neck, and they were all covered by the goo. But he looked fine otherwise.

I didn't say anything, but I wasn't sure if it was only the saliva of the dead things or contact with any bodily fluids that leaked from them that spread the virus. So I was more than a little worried Andy might have been infected. The radio reports from the government hadn't specified if a simple scratch was an issue or not. We would have to quarantine him when we got back home, but I worried more about him becoming one of those monsters.

Randy joined us about that time, and he gave me a knowing look about the scratches but kept his mouth shut. He had two large duffle bags stuffed with all manner of medication. If we secured enough water and additional supplies, I'd call it a successful mission.

We were able to pull all the water and soda out of the store, including the back room. It looked like they had recently received a shipment and we took it all. We also cleared out the other useful items in the store: canned goods, OTC painkillers, hygiene products, and some toys for the kids. I had to; their childhoods had just been ripped from them and they needed something to make them smile.

We filled the trucks to capacity in a few minutes and grabbed the keys from the wheels. It was time to go home!

Andy started to get into the cab with me, but I locked the doors, stopping him cold.

"What the hell are you doing? Let me in! I want to go home and I'm not in the mood for this shit!" Andy yelled.

I felt bad for him, I did, but he smelled so bad that I just couldn't let him in the cab with me. I powered down the window about an inch and told him, "You have to sit in the back, with the stuff. You stink, terrible."

Randy was watching the drama unfold and soon my walkie-talkie came to life. "You're being kind of a jerk, you realize that, right?"

"You're just mad about the Billy The Kid comment. You wouldn't let him in either," I replied.

As I set the radio down, a small object skipped across the hood of the truck. It only took about five seconds to realize what it was.

I unlocked the door and yelled at Andy to get in just as he ducked for cover. Someone had just shot at us and I couldn't determine their location. I sure wasn't going to wait to find out. They had us in their sights and at a disadvantage; it was time to bug-out.

No more shots were fired as we exited the parking lot. I figured the person or persons that had been working on getting into the controlled substance safe had returned. The shot must have been intended to get us out of the area, allowing them to resume their work on the safe. That was fine with me, but they sure as hell didn't need to shoot at us to get us to move.

Chapter 17:
Home and Gone Again

When we got back, it played out exactly as I had expected. Because of the scratches and us not knowing how, other than a bite, the virus spread, they placed Andy in quarantine. He wasn't happy and his wife was flat-out unhinged about it. They had three small children, and she was not thrilled about being left alone with them for seventy-two hours, during the end of the world.

I'm not sure how we landed on seventy-two hours, although it seemed like a sufficient amount of time for any infections to take hold. I can tell you this, the way he smelled was enough to get him locked away for the next year!

After being checked, the rest of us continued to the community supply depot. It was simply one of the empty homes, but *supply depot* sounds much better. We unloaded the supplies and made sure Pat got her hands on the medicine we'd secured. I wanted it in her hands so she could determine who needed which medication.

Now, I'm not saying she's a busybody, but she knows A LOT about the people in our community! I'm positive she could recite, off the top of her head, the medications taken by fifty percent of our community.

After we finished, I realized that I needed to clear my head, so I walked home. I searched my pack for the Reese's Cups I'd taken from the drugstore and stashed away for Darline. They're one of her favorites, and the end of the world has been hard on all of us. So a little happy surprise was in order. I prepared myself to be asked why I didn't get some cake... she really loves cake! But Reese's Cups would have to suffice today.

As I unlocked the door, I stuck my head through the opening and announced myself so I didn't get shot. I was happy to be home and looked forward to surprising Darline with the Reese's. The past three weeks felt like an immeasurable torrent of agonizing work that was breaking my back. And, as I pointed out, I'm *around* fifty years old, so I needed a break and needed one badly.

I entered after realizing that no bullets were coming in my direction and I had no holes in my body. Darline was talking to someone, but because I only heard her voice, I figured she was on her cell or the walkie-talkie and we had no unwelcome visitors.

I yelled a hello, and she immediately came downstairs. When she got to the first floor, she handed me the walkie-talkie and told me it was my brother, Stone. She grabbed me and whispered, "I missed you, but you need to talk to Stone, now."

Her urgency and insistence wasn't right, not at all. I grabbed the walkie-talkie from her and as I pressed the talk button, I handed her the snacks I'd lifted from the drugstore. Her smile passed too quickly, and her excitement was much too subdued, which told me something had gone sideways with Stone.

"What's up, my brother?" He didn't respond. Then Stone and Darline said, in unison, "You need to say over when you're having a serious conversation on a walkie-talkie." I winced at the double-barrelled verbal assault and then pressed the talk button and said, "Over."

Darline rolled her eyes and walked away. I could hear her packing up a bag or something, and I was puzzled as to why.

Stone told me his community had fallen after one of his residents had gone on a supply run and became infected. They followed their re-entry protocols but hadn't detected the wound.

"I need help, brother. I'm on the second floor of the house with Kit. We have enough ammo and guns with us to mount a decent defense. But not for long, because it's spreading like a ten-cent prostitute."

Kit yelled at Stone, and it made me smile. Not sure why, it just did. Maybe it was the normalcy of her reaction in a crazy world. Or that things hadn't gotten so bad that she wouldn't scold him. Don't know, don't care, it made me smile.

Stone mumbled something and came back on the walkie-talkie. "We also have food for up to three days. They haven't breached our house, but there's enough of those things running around that loading our SUV and evacuating without cover will be impossible..."

I cut him off and told him I would be there inside of thirty minutes. "Just get the stuff staged on the first floor so we can start loading as soon as I pull in your driveway." Then I followed up a few seconds later by saying, "Over."

Stone came back on the walkie-talkie with some complicated news. "Hey, you remember the strategy we talked about with the barricades, right? Well, we implemented them with one little change. We ended up using a slide lock to secure the vehicle entrance, a huge slide lock... over."

I chewed on that information for a second. It wasn't good news. With a standard padlock and chain, I could shoot the lock, cut the lock, or cut the chain. With a slide lock, I wouldn't even have access to the lock from outside the gate.

"Okay, did you get the CONEX containers for the wall?"

Nothing came back.

"Sorry, I forgot... over."

"Yes, the main access points are a combination of CONEX containers, jersey barriers, and cyclone fencing. All strung with so much razor wire you'll cut your hand off simply thinking about climbing it... over."

I smiled because I know my brother, and I can guarantee that he wasn't exaggerating. That fence would be covered from top to bottom in razor wire.

"Where are they congregating, or are they even congregating?" I asked that question because of what we'd seen at the airport. I yelled "OVER" because it was getting on my last nerve that I kept forgetting to say over.

He told me they were just wandering in groups and trying to find stimuli. I figured he meant food. He said the search for stimuli was leading them to the fence because a convoy of military vehicles had passed by an hour ago. The noise drew them closer to the fence for a better look. Since then they had been wandering around the area with no focus.

What he told me next was really bad news. "Unfortunately, that puts them by the main entrance. Those Bradleys and Humvees were loud. They got the attention of every shambling thing within a mile. And, well, now they're searching for that convoy. It's like they realize they have food inside, over."

This bit of news put me in a salty mood. First, we are not food; we are the top of the food chain. Second, how the hell would I get those doors open and get past the things crowding the gate? Third, what about the things shambling outside, waiting for some dumbass like me to stop in the middle of the street?

"Stone, is anyone else with you and Kit? We have room, and we could use the additional bodies around the community, over."

I wasn't sure if what we'd built was a compound, a village, or more like a last stand. It was becoming clear that whatever it was, we needed to hold onto it by any means necessary.

His stark response rattled me. "We're all that's left, brother, and I will have to kill all of my neighbors to get you in and us out."

I couldn't find any words. His group had stood about eighty strong, and he'd had some tough people with him. The virus was proving to be ruthless and starting to appear unstoppable.

Darline snapped me out of my stupor. "He didn't say over, please tell him to say over. I don't want to hear anymore." I spun to face her, and she continued, "We're going to get your brother and Kit. I'm going with you because… just because! Do you understand me? I'm going just because!" She visibly shook with a mixture of anger and fear.

"Got it," I replied, just as Stone said, "Over."

We got busy and came up with a plan. It would work like this: When we got about a mile away, Stone would start thinning the herd. He would initially focus on the ones outside the fence, giving us some space to work. While we worked the gate, he'd put rounds into the ones inside the fence, creating a path to his house.

We knew that even with his suppressed AR, he would draw attention to his position. He would only be able to clean up a limited number before drawing the entire herd to his front door. That wouldn't be much of a help while we loaded our vehicles, he and Kit, and tried to leave. So he would create a diversion to draw them from the gate. I didn't know what it would be, but I couldn't help but think it would involve Tannerite. My brother has some very cool toys; they weren't Randy's C4, but they were very cool.

Chapter 18:
Some Time At Home

As we packed, the door opened and Lisa announced herself. She's one of Darline's best friends. I'm not a fan. She's loud and built better than most lightweight boxing champs. Sporting a high and tight, she's easily mistaken for a man, from a distance, that is. I'll give you five dollars if you tell her that, because she's a brute and wouldn't hesitate to throat punch you.

She was geared up with multiple weapons and asked when we were heading out to get Stone. I looked at Darline, who wouldn't make eye contact with me.

"Ummm, someone want to tell me what's going on?" Still nothing from Darline, and Lisa began catching on that I was not, in the slightest, aware she was joining us.

"Look, Darline called me and asked me to help. She tried Randy, but he's passed out, Al is no spring chicken, Dillan is working the gate, and Tesha is looking after her little one. I was the next person on the list." Lisa looked at Darline and said, "We'll talk about my rank on your list later."

I continued staring at Darline as she found other things to do to avoid making eye contact with me. Getting nowhere with Darline, I addressed Lisa. "Thank you for offering to help, but this is my brother, not our community, and this is going to be a dangerous trip, Lisa. We might all get eaten and I can't ask you to go." I was getting ready to launch into part two of my diatribe when she cut me off.

"Hey, you don't have permission to tell me what to do, not even once. I fought my way home from downtown. I started killing them before you even had your windows boarded up, JACK, so shut up, load up, and let's get moving. Your brother can't hold out forever."

I mentioned Lisa was loud, right? But I couldn't argue the fact that my brother needed us, now. So I nodded and said okay, because she kind of intimidates me, and she's so loud when she gets worked up. It was easier to just go with it; she might even be an asset.

We packed up in ten minutes and touched base with Stone as we hit the road. The situation was holding, but I took notice of the anxiety in his voice. He needed help, ASAP.

We'd loaded up heavy on ammo and blunt force weapons because something told me this fight would get up close and personal. I think Lisa was secretly looking forward to some up-close fighting; she's an angry, angry person. She held a large knife and had a glint in her eye and a crooked smile on her face that would have made me uncomfortable if she was my girlfriend or wife. Like she was imagining cutting off my manhood, just to see what it would be like.

We exited the main gate in my Grand Cherokee, geared up for the fight coming our way. Dillan told me the channel he and the other guards used. He let us know that if we got hung up, we were to radio them. He would split off with whoever was available and have our backs within fifteen minutes.

I leaned in close and told him to keep his walkie-talkie charged because this one could bounce off the rails fast. Lisa made a point of saying goodbye to Dillan, in her usual gregarious style, and let her smile and stare linger longer than I felt was normal for a regular goodbye.

From the rearview mirror I watched Lisa watching Dillan when she noticed me watching her watching Dillan. I've never seen a face turn from an expression of infatuation and all smiles to *I'll rip your face off* more quickly in my life. She raised her eyebrows and bugged her eyes and yelled, "WHAT."

I smiled and responded, "Oh, nothing."

"Darline, is your husband always this annoying?" Lisa asked and Darline didn't skip a beat.

"Yes, yes he is."

I loved that I had pushed her buttons. Then I decided to throw caution to the wind with a little song that goes something like this, "Lisa and Dillan sittin' in a tree…"

I was interrupted by two assaults on my body. A gut shot from my wife and a head shot from the backseat. But, even though Lisa worked up a good amount of energy and hit me square on the side of my head, it was worth it.

My amusement didn't help calm things down and Darline finally made me apologize. But I whispered, "Not sorry" under my breath. At the end of the day, I'm but a child trapped in a man's body!

As we traversed the side streets on the way to my brother's house, one thing became clear. A lot of people had fought for their lives in the streets of our city and many of them lost that fight.

We observed other communities, like ours, had sprung up, giving me hope we could beat this and keep the world from ending.

We saw several dozen of the things during our trek but managed to avoid engaging them. They were definitely attracted to noise and would try to follow us in that shambling, stumbling walk they did. I found it unnerving to watch them as they chased us, or I should say as they chased the food in the Jeep.

A pattern started presenting itself. On several streets, any remnants of battle had been cleaned up. Piles of debris and burn pits marked the starting point at about a block before signs of a compound or encampment. It was good to see humanity refused to lay down and die.

I smiled at the thought that living in RAM was the reason we were all still alive. We made a note to contact these communities at a later date. Establishing trade and joining forces would be essential for our survival and the survival of humanity as a whole.

We were about two miles from Stone's compound

when we came upon a military blockade. Jersey barriers and sandbags blocked the road, along with what I assumed to be one of the Bradley Fighting Vehicles Stone had talked about. They had positioned it behind the makeshift wall with two Humvees, fitted with turret guns, flanking it.

No soldiers, other than the turret gunners, were visible outside the battlewagons. As we approached, no soldiers exited the vehicles, but their turrets adjusted in our direction. Looking down the barrel of the Bradley's 25mm chain gun was not a comforting feeling, so I slowed to a stop.

Bradleys come armed with enough firepower to rip our vehicle and its occupants apart. The TOW missiles they carried would, in fact, obliterate my Jeep. I gave that some thought and realized that with the amount of grief the Jeep had caused me over the last year, and the money spent fixing all of that grief, it might be fun to watch it eradicated. But only after we were no longer sitting in it.

Both Humvees had M2s mounted; those are .50 cal full auto machine guns, affectionately referred to as Ma-Deuces. They're capable of sending a lot of enormous bullets at you at virtually the same time. I only had one of the M4s I'd taken from Westley's house, and the ladies had ARs and handguns. It would be a one-sided fight if it turned into that. I had no intention of letting that happen and started backing away.

When I did that, one of the turret gunners put a hand up making a STOP motion. My stomach clenched tight at the order, but he didn't seem threatening and something about the soldier looked vaguely familiar.

He talked into his shoulder mic and then listened for a second. He waved us forward after his conversation ended. I couldn't put my finger on it, but I couldn't shake the feeling I had seen him before.

When Willis's head popped out of the Bradley's turret, it hit me. The Humvee gunner was one of the soldiers from the airport; he looked worn out, but still managed a smile.

Willis exited the Bradley, and he was as big as I remembered, and his smile still reached his eyes. I wasn't sure what he was smiling about, but I took it as a good sign. A sign that he might not shoot us.

He waved us over but told us to stay in the Jeep and pull as close to the barricade as possible. I noticed that he exited and walked directly in front of the Bradley, keeping his back tight against its armor, like he was trying to block an attack from the rear. The move made me uneasy. He directed us to pull sidelong to the barricade, and in as tight as I could get.

"Mr. Otto, the apocalypse is only three weeks old, and I've seen you twice, and I have to say I'm relieved to see you alive."

His smile never left his face, but his eyes clouded with worry when he told me he was relieved to see I was alive. Things must be getting tough, and I asked him just that.

"What's the good word, Sergeant Willis? Oh, and it's good to see you and your men. I'm still alive because of you. If I didn't tell you at the airport, I'm telling you now, thank you."

Darline leaned over and thanked him. She said something along the lines of me being a pain-in-the-ass. However, I was her pain-in-the-ass, and she was thankful I got to keep being her pain. It was a backhanded compliment, only with a fully closed fist… that thumped me in the face. Willis chuckled while tipping his helmet to her.

After the moment of brevity, his eyes clouded up again, and his face became stony. He leaned in a bit and asked, "How are you and your group holding up? Have you lost anyone to the virus in the last few weeks?"

As he spoke, the turret gunners scanned the surrounding area. It was obvious they were waiting for something to happen and it was making me a nervous wreck.

Lisa hit the back of my seat and said, "By the way, my name is Lisa. I'm sure it was just an oversight that Darline's pain-in-the-ass didn't introduce me."

I face palmed.

Willis looked into the back and nodded, "Ma'am, I'm Sergeant Willis."

Being referred to as *ma'am* appeared to do a number on Lisa, causing her to go silent for a moment, but only for a moment. Then the muttering started. "Ma'am? I'll give you a ma'am upside that little boy face of yours. Lucky you got that gun, little man."

I found too much pleasure in Lisa's distress. I am but a child!

Willis asked me to step out for a private conversation. I didn't object. Sensing the seriousness of the situation, no one else in the Jeep did either. We walked to the front of the Bradley but far enough away from the Jeep to have privacy before he started.

"Where're you going with a mil-spec M4 and two other people geared up for Armageddon?"

The question snapped me back to the urgency of the situation. I'd gotten distracted by the large gun pointing at me when we approached the roadblock.

"Willis, I need to get to my brother; his community has been overrun…"

Willis stopped me. "By the living or the dead?"

The question caught me off guard. "By the dead. What's going on that you asked me that question? The one about the living or the dead, are we already devolving to that?"

Willis cut a hard look at the Jeep and informed me that what I was about to hear wasn't confirmed and might be classified.

"We've had some reports of rogue BSU forces doing shoot and scoots. One, maybe two shots at people and then retreating into deep cover. We've also seen a surge in the dead that doesn't line up with the region's population. We don't know if the two are related, but it's looking like they are."

My face telegraphed my shock when I connected the dots to the incident at the drug store.

"What? What happened, Otto?" Willis asked.

"We went on a small supply run, first one since this started, to pick up some medications and water from a drugstore. Someone fired on us, only one poorly placed shot. They had us dead to rights and could have easily picked us off. We thought they were trying to push us off so they could get to the heavier narcotics. We were happy to oblige. I thought it was odd they didn't at least take another shot. Unless, that is, they never intended to stand and fight, or get to the drugs, for that matter."

Willis pulled a map from his tactical vest and asked me to pinpoint the location of the store. I showed him the location and the area we believed the shot came from. He quickly radioed in the coordinates and then barked off a series of commands. Within seconds a Black Hawk raced through the sky, heading in the direction I had just given Willis. Something was happening and happening too close to my home. The question was why. Why would they be doing this when they have much bigger problems in BSU?

The fact that there was zero civilian gun ownership means it was government sanctioned. They'd be using either BSU troops or civilians with government-issued weapons. But why? Something bigger was happening.

I asked Willis to hold tight and ran to the Jeep. Leaning in, I told Darline, "Get Dillan on the radio and tell him to increase the guards at the gate, along the fence, and the foot patrols inside the perimeter. Also, tell him to start scanning the trees. I can't tell him more because I don't have any more information."

I turned to walk away, about-faced and added, "Let him know the Black Hawk that he'll see shortly is friendly, so don't shoot it. Let them land if they need a place to operate."

Now I walked away and stayed away. As I did, I heard her on the walkie-talkie contacting Dillan. I also heard Lisa asking if she could talk to Dillan... that'll be hard to get used to.

I rejoined Willis as he was folding up the map. He turned to me and said, "Look, we can't let you travel past this point. The area is hot with the dead and it's getting worse by the minute. We've been hitting them hard, but they just keep showing up. Like someone's shipping them to us."

Already shaking my head after he said, *Can't let you travel*, I turned to walk away when Willis put one of his *boy giant* hands on my shoulder to turn me around. I slipped it and kept walking.

"Come on, man!" he yelled with a hint of exasperation seeping into his voice. "My last three weeks have sucked. Please, don't turn this into something it doesn't have to be, just listen to me... please."

The sincerity in his voice stopped me in my tracks, I had to understand where he was coming from. I was putting him, his men, Darline, and Lisa at risk. But I couldn't let Stone and Kit die trapped in his house. That image terrified me.

So I employed the only job skill I possess that's useful during the apocalypse; I negotiated.

"Willis," I started, "what if you split one of the Humvees off and send it with me? That way, your squad can keep an eye on me. Make sure I don't wander into any hot zones and help rescue my brother."

I should have asked for the Bradley, giving him room to negotiate me down to a Humvee. But the pressure and urgency of the situation had me a little off my game.

Willis seemed surprised by the tactic. I'm sure he wasn't accustomed to negotiating with the men under his command. The military is more *do as I say…* especially in times of war and zombie apocalypses.

"You're a pain in my ass, you know that, right?"

I responded with the truth, "It usually takes people a little longer to figure it out, but I am a pain-in-the-ass." I'm not sure he saw the humor, but it sure brought a grin to his man boy face.

"We're forming extraction teams now to get people who haven't set up communities to safety. And we've accepted the fact that civilians will need to take an active role on the teams. We may be able to use this as a guide for the missions to come. Because I have a feeling we'll be working with more pain-in-the-ass people soon enough. It'll be a good experience for the squad."

The mischievous look on his face told me he was going against someone's orders, and that was fine with me. He retreated to the Bradley, with his head on a swivel, making me nervous enough to do the same thing. Although, I didn't understand why or what I was looking for. Something bad was happening, and it made me exceedingly anxious.

Chapter 19: The Big Guns

Willis brought me over to a Humvee with Lewis and Stevenson inside. No first names for these two. I was good with it because they were fully kitted out and battle tested. That's all I needed to know.

We reviewed the strategy and tactics that Stone and I had in place. They liked parts of the strategy, but not all of it.

We decided to let Stone handle the monsters inside the fence. However, the Humvee would be used as a battering ram to move, disable, and kill the ones outside the gate, allowing Stone to focus solely on the things inside the fence. We wanted to avoid drawing too much attention to ourselves and would keep Ma-Deuce quiet unless we had no choice.

The Humvee would approach first while we hung back and waited for the signal to advance. Lewis and Stevenson planned to use breaching charges on the hinges of the CONEX entry point and then pull the door clear. They would kill anything inside the CONEX, allowing us to roll through. The Humvee wouldn't fit through the container with the turret, so they would cover the entry and neutralize all external threats.

Easy-peasy... right??

We radioed Stone and told him the plan and told him to start thinning inside the fence. He should activate the distractions once the Humvee made contact with the things outside the gate. He was ready!

This *mission* would tax both groups. We were asking trained soldiers to work in conjunction with two weekend warriors, their wives, and a very loud friend. What could go wrong?

We arrived at the hold point for the Jeep and Lewis reviewed the plan one more time. He stressed with me that we needed to move when given the signal and follow the plan to the letter. Keep our radios on and heads on a swivel when we got past the gate.

He looked me in the eyes and said, "You got this! Let's get your brother and his wife and EVAC in fifteen minutes. And you radio us the very second you think you have a problem... you clear on that?"

"Crystal," I replied.

With a big smile and a *hooyah* he headed to the gate.

From my position I had eyes on Stone's house and the upstairs room where he and Kit were holed up. I couldn't see the damage he'd inflicted as he poured round after round into the unseen herd from his perch. Access to his community was on a side street flanked by small, one-story strip malls on either side. The CONEX gate sat between the strip malls with large fenced-off gaps on either side. And

147

yes, the fencing was completely covered in razor wire.

The houses started about fifty yards after the buildings and their parking lots. This setup gave Stone excellent lines of fire for thinning the herd. Unfortunately, it would block our line of sight when we breached the gate. No turning back now; we just needed to make it work!

Roughly twenty things (we really needed to find a name for them) shuffled around our side of the gate. Their focus was on getting past the gate and they became more and more agitated as Stone killed the ones on his side.

It was the first time I'd witnessed them act this way. They pulled at the gate, not with any kind of force but still working at it, while giving off loud raspy groans. Up until now they had only shown the most basic motor skills, and no vocalization. The sound was disturbing, like wet sandpaper against hollow PVC pipe. Some tried getting past the razor wire and were cut to ribbons as they pulled at it. Yet they still worked at getting past it. This behavior was an alarming development, but I didn't have time to be distracted by it. We were getting ready to fight.

The Humvee picked up speed as it approached the CONEX gate, heading directly for the group blocking our entry. When the Humvee's brush guard plowed into the group, Stone broke over the radio confirming he was starting the distraction. Two seconds later, an enormous explosion, then another, sounded from inside the fence. I could see large columns of smoke at the opposite end of the community. Some of the things started moving toward the explosions. Then a third explosion sounded and with it more of the things joined the others bent on investigating the sounds.

The things inside the fence weren't as animated as the ones outside. I made a mental note that I needed to observe them much closer in the weeks to come. Something was happening to them, something that made me uncomfortable.

The Humvee had cleared a path with its first pass and began coming around for another when it connected with a dense cluster of things. The Humvee pitched hard right while scattering broken bodies in every direction. With the monsters cleared from the area, the reason for the hard hit and ricochet became clear. They had clustered around a ground level electrical transformer while devouring a badly decomposed corpse. They'd eaten most of the corpse to the bone like vultures stripping an animal carcass. I will never get used to this!

The Humvee had only taken a glancing blow, but it was hard enough for it to stall out. Lewis attempted to restart the diesel with no luck and the racket began drawing a crowd.

Stevenson appeared in the turret and surveyed the area. A large, previously unseen gaggle of monsters shambled from behind the Humvee and began closing on them, fast.

Lewis broke over the radio. "She's being a little cranky and won't turn over. She gets like this from time to time. My girl's getting old. We need a few minutes to let her figure it out. Can you put some rounds into the group to our six? It'll draw them towards you and buy us a few minutes to get the old girl running. We need to keep the big gun quiet until we need it. Can't risk bringing any more out of hiding… over."

I didn't like the idea of being used as bait. However, I didn't have time to question it. We needed to get that vehicle back in the fight before the dead lost interest in the diversion Stone had created.

I responded by opening the sunroof, climbing out waist-high and lining up a shot. The things heading toward the Humvee were dressed in wait staff and kitchen clothing. Both the clothing and the skin of the pack leaders had been shredded. The cause of the damage became obvious a moment later. The restaurant they had been working in sat directly behind them as they marched towards the Humvee. It was the dinner rush, and it was rushing at the Humvee!

When I put my eye to the scope of my M4, I could see that a large window fronting the restaurant was shattered. Tattered bits of uniforms and skin were hanging from the sides and top of the now windowless opening.

Along the bottom, bodies, some still moving, lay across the jagged cavity. It appeared they had been used as a sick human threshold as others exited the restaurant through the window. The blood from the threshold bodies poured down the frame and pooled on the sidewalk. Broken bones, from arms and legs, had ripped through the flesh that once

B.D. Lutz

covered them. Some still tried to move mangled limbs while others were lucky enough to have had their brains ground into the sidewalk.

Lewis broke over the radio. "Are you going to actually pull the trigger, or just stare at them?"

His voice snapped me back to the task at hand. I settled on a target and pulled the trigger. The M4 fired three rounds within a second and the recoil pulled me off target. That was no way to discover the fire selector was positioned to a three-round-burst.

I managed to hit one in the shoulder, slamming it to the ground and taking two more with it. It wouldn't stop them, but it slowed them down enough for me to switch the selector to semi-auto and adjust my aim. This was going to take some getting used to and I started to miss my Ruger.

I lined up a nasty-looking thing with a full sleeve tattoo, greased-over high-n-tight haircut, and a full beard. He looked like he'd spent his days at the gym and nights strutting around like a gift to all women. You know the type; they've declared they have life all figured out. They treat you like they feel bad for you because you're not as *enlightened* as them. Smirking when you're off on your pronunciation of Caprese. Advising you on what to eat so you can look just like him because he's perfect. I'm betting this one couldn't even change a flat tire. I kind of enjoyed putting the 5.56 projectile through his half-eaten head.

After shooting another one, it seemed to do the trick in redirecting the group away from Lewis and Stevenson.

Darline grabbed my leg to get my attention. She handed me the radio and told me that Stone needed to talk to me.

"What's up?" I asked and followed up with "OVER" several seconds later.

"What's happening out there? Are you in trouble or just having too much fun with what appears to be a mil-spec M4?"

I looked toward his house and found him in the window with binoculars pointed at me. I waved; he didn't wave back.

"We ran into a little delay with the Humvee…"

He cut me off. "Well, I don't want to sound ungrateful. But my distraction won't work forever, and your shooting is drawing them back to your position. You're going to end up fighting your way to the house."

Well shit, this was heading south fast. "Do you have more distractions set up, anything to draw them away from the gate? Also, you didn't say over."

He didn't see the humor and I think I saw him flip me off from the window.

"I have one more. But it's intended to be a defensive asset, not a distraction like the others. Meaning it'll be hard to hit from my window. Oh, and it has a couple of pounds of shrapnel mixed in with it. You'll all need to take cover before I set it off."

I replied, "Go for it, Stone." I looked toward the Hummer. "Lewis, get Stevenson in the cab."

"Already on it, I was listening in."

He'd no sooner finished speaking when Stone hit the device... *Nice shooting, my brother!*

The shrapnel ripped through the air, obliterating four monsters in the process. Some shrapnel made it to the road, falling harmlessly around us.

We sat about sixty yards from the Humvee and hadn't been paying attention to the dead wait staff. They had halved the distance and were closing fast. I needed to thin them out in case they managed to make it to our position. My confidence in the Jeep's ability to pull free of them, without causing catastrophic damage, was low. If we got trapped inside the Jeep, the entire plan would fall apart and we'd all die.

The Humvee roared to life and started moving as I took my first shot. It was headed directly at us while increasing its speed. Lewis' face and the brush guard were all that were visible. The giant vehicle remained on course and I feared it would plow directly into the Jeep.

In full-blown panic I screamed, "This isn't part of the plan."

I watched as Lewis pulled alongside the pack of things advancing on us. I jumped back inside the Jeep and braced for the inevitable impact. Lewis cut the Humvee hard right, smashing the front line of the monsters. The sounds of breaking bones and internal organs bursting was sickening. Blood exploded from the herd, covering the Jeep, as the huge vehicle bounced over the dead wait staff.

The next thing I heard was Lewis on the radio telling

me to get ready to execute the plan. I needed to ensure Lewis and Stevenson would have time to breach the CONEX entrance. *Time to kill the stragglers.*

I again exited through the sunroof and took aim at the three remaining things headed our way. It was quick work as they had stopped moving toward us and seemed confused about which vehicle to pursue. So I cleared up the confusion for them and put them down in quick order.

At the same time, Lewis finished what he'd started and demolished the ones loitering by the entrance. He drove to the front of the container and exited the Humvee in a flash. Stevenson sat in the turret slowly sweeping the area while Lewis positioned the breaching charge. He ran with the detonation cord back to the Humvee, pulled several feet away, and an explosion soon followed.

Working together, they wedged a pry bar into the breached door and pulled back, giving themselves access to the locking mechanism and allowing them to disable it, free the door, and drag it out of the way. It was impressive to watch them work. And it made me realize that Darline, Lisa and I could not have done this without them.

We were moving as the door pulled free of the opening. I burst through the CONEX before realizing I was scared to death. Everything that could go wrong played like a movie in my head. "Stone, get moving, we're on our way."

He replied, "On it."

We arrived at his house in less than thirty seconds and hit no resistance along the way. We had a simple plan. I would help Stone and Kit load up the vehicles while Darline and Lisa covered our backs.

They took cover in some shrubs that offered excellent concealment from the surrounding area. They stationed themselves about twenty feet from our makeshift loading zone, giving themselves an ample field of view.

Unfortunately, the noise we made while entering the community had already garnered the attention of the things Stone had distracted. We needed to move like lightning if we wanted to avoid getting killed.

Lewis and Stevenson kept the gate clear for our exit. However, we had a lot to accomplish before we needed to worry about exiting.

We worked fast; Stone was waiting at the back door with his first load when we pulled in. He ran past me as I ran into his house. Kit began getting the cargo ready to hand off to us. We moved like the wind and had already started loading the Jeep when the first shot came from the front of the house. I ducked, instinctively, looking in the direction the shots came from.

Darline yelled, "We're running out of time. They've lost interest in whatever was keeping them at the end of the street. It's going to get very loud, very quickly, so move ass, people."

Move ass, people??? She's a little brute.

We loaded the last of the items and called to Lisa and Darline when all hell broke loose... we were out of time. I grabbed my M4 and started to the front of the house; we needed to ensure we didn't get overrun while we headed back to the gate. With two, fully loaded SUVs in our little caravan, we would be an easy target. I needed to identify the direction they were traveling from and ensure our path was clear, allowing a trouble-free egress.

When I reached Lisa and Darline, they were out from cover and working on thinning the herd. Only several of the monsters suffered headshots. The rest, about eight, lay immobilized with shots to the legs and hips. It was a solid tactic, allowing them to neutralize targets more quickly because they didn't have to focus on headshots.

These things may not die when they're supposed to. But, their bodies have to obey the laws of physics. In other words, their motion was being stopped by the force of a bullet. Also, shattered knees and hips cannot support a body, forcing that body to crawl and crawling is much slower than walking. I loved this tactic.

I joined in for a few rounds, but I realized we needed to get moving. With the noise and movement, we would bring all the remaining inhabitants to our location.

We retreated to the SUVs as more of them started approaching from across the street. It looked like we'd make it out, but it would be close.

We started to back out of Stone's drive and I advised Lewis and Stevenson we were on our way when we heard it. A piercing scream from across the street, followed by a woman bolting from her house and running in our direction. Dozens of things emerged from behind her home in pursuit. It was going to be close for her.

We were screaming for her to run and started to ready our weapons to provide covering fire when she suddenly slammed to the ground. She'd unwittingly rushed into the arms of one of the immobilized zombies.

Her face hit the pavement so hard that blood splattered from the sides of her head and cut off her scream. Stone opened fire on the thing that had pulled her to the ground, but it was too late. It had already peeled away a large chunk of her calf when the bullet found the top of its head.

Within seconds, the dead covered her and started pulling her apart. Still alive when her mutilation started, Stone put a round through her head and ended her suffering.

Lisa and Darline went deafeningly silent as we drove towards the exit. I didn't need to ask them why; I had the same thought running around my head. Had we killed that one, instead of disabling it, that woman may still be alive. This would be one of many tragedies we would live with for the rest of our lives. How would we return to normal when this all ended, if it ever ended?

We met up with Lewis and Stevenson who had been busy defending the gate. I counted about fifteen more dead things scattered about signaling that the activity had picked up.

Stone and I stood watch as Lewis and Stevenson re-secured the gate, the hope being it would keep the ones inside the fence from becoming a problem outside.

While they worked on it, I asked Stevenson why they used the M2 and not something with more accuracy?

He smiled and said, "Have you ever witnessed the result of being shot by a .50 cal high velocity round? Well, you probably haven't, but I can tell you, you don't need to aim for the head, just the body. That round will literally rip a person apart, so even if they don't die, they're out of the fight." That made perfect sense, and it was the same tactic we had used earlier.

I think he sensed my unease when he finished because he leaned in close and said, "Look, we saw what happened. We were getting ready, just like you, to lay down covering fire. You can't help what happened, and the question is why did she wait so long to run for help? The area had been clear of UCs for plenty-long-enough for her to have made it to you. You all did the right thing when you started to immobilize them. They would have overrun your position if you hadn't. Get it out of your head that you caused her death."

I felt a little better after he said that, and I hoped Lisa and Darline heard him. I was walking away when I realized that he called the things UCs.

"You called them UCs. What's that stand for?"

Stevenson looked a little surprised by my question. "Undead corpse. They started calling them that about two weeks ago. It's an accurate description. It removes all doubt that they're dead and should be made dead again. We lost a lot of troops because they were still looking at them as RAM citizens and couldn't pull the trigger. The description was the start of a campaign to ensure we treated them appropriately, like an enemy. It's been a little tough to transition to; we still catch ourselves calling them things."

I liked it and decided we had finally found the name for what we had been calling *those things*.

We met up with Willis back at the roadblock and told him what had happened… or debriefed him, as he called it. He seemed happy with the INTEL. He planned to use it to put together a report on integrating civilians into search and rescue and other missions, easing the military's load – a military that was quickly becoming overwhelmed and stretched thin and needed the help.

He pulled me aside and asked if I remembered what we'd talked about at the airport: the plan to arm the remaining population with military weapons and machines. I, most assuredly, did! He said he would visit the community and review how the program would work. I couldn't contain myself, but I tried. I answered much faster than I intended to: "Yes… yes, we want in!"

CHAPTER 20:
A SLOW SHIP ON ERIE

TWO WEEKS EARLIER

The water was calm on this beautiful summer day on Lake Erie. The tug pushing the modified flat-top barge experienced no issues today. It would be a smooth run from the port of Buffalo, NY to Edgewater Beach on the shore of Cleveland, OH.

This marked Captain Riggins' second run between the two cities, and he could get used to it. It got him away from the nightmare his life had become, away from the loss of his family, *all* of his family. Except for his lone surviving crew member, John Hettinger, every single person he had known was dead.

The BSU government created this opportunity for him. He got food, medical care, and a place to live inside one of the last safe places in Blue States United.

Memories of pleading with his wife to move to RAM inevitably flooded his mind this time of day. He was getting hungry and with that came the angry thoughts of how it all played out. How his wife wanted to stay close to her family that were all bleeding-heart liberals. How she begged him to stay and how he relented. She and his children would probably still be alive had they moved, had he just forced them to move.

If he could eat something, he'd feel better, but the stench coming from the "cargo" made him gag at the thought of eating. No, he'd be waiting to eat until halfway through the return trip.

He directed his anger at everyone. The BSU for letting it get this bad. The dumbasses didn't even try to stop the virus. They tried to include them, reason with them and make them part of society. But they didn't try to stop it until it was too late.

Anger with RAM for building that damn wall that stopped so many people living in BSU from finding safety when they fled their homes and tried to enter RAM.

They all needed to suffer his anger and rage, and this allowed him a way to get at least one side to pay the price. He'd figure out a way for BSU to pay, and when the time came, they would pay dearly for what they did to his family.

As he lost himself in thoughts of revenge and the deep sadness that accompanied memories of his family, Hettinger leaned into the wheelhouse and told him the city skyline had come into view and they should adjust their course for the cargo destination.

"Thanks John, I'll adjust Starboard in three minutes."

John didn't like the change he'd seen in the captain these last two weeks. He'd become absent from his body and mind. He didn't follow protocols, something he had been a stickler for in all the years John had sailed with him. Riggins' eyes burned with an anger which, at times, scared him. He'd taken to zoning out while at the helm, something John would have to talk to him about. He just didn't know how.

John and the captain's political beliefs differed greatly, but he respected and liked him. The captain was a hardworking, honest man who had loved his family more than life itself. John was an only child and lost his parents years ago. But the captain became his family the day he started working for him. He was all that John had left.

John and the captain had lived offshore since two weeks into the meltdown. John had fought his way to the captain's house, which was about four miles from his apartment. The carnage he witnessed on his way terrified him. People ran wild in the streets, ripping each other apart and eating one another.

He saw a man with a shopping cart full of electronics, not food or water but a TV and smart phones. As the looter tried to dodge the infected, he'd tripped over a freshly severed arm. The cart careened forward while the man slammed to the pavement.

When he lifted his head, he revealed to John a mouth full of missing and ruined teeth, some reduced to tiny ivory-colored nubs. John pulled over to help when one of the infected plowed into the man, taking him back to the ground. John exited his car in time to witness the man's eyes being torn from their sockets and eaten. He stumbled backwards in horror. The man screamed for help as the thing peeled his face off and ate it. It haunted John to this day. He took four undead lives that morning but made it to the captain.

They lived by scavenging all the watercraft they found either adrift in the harbor or abandoned at the dock. He knew it wouldn't last, and it didn't. That was how they'd ended up here.

They were preparing to make their first supply run on land when the government finally showed up and made them an offer. The offer was simple enough. They would take the *cargo* to different locations in RAM, and in return they'd get to eat and sleep safely at night. The only issues were that the cargo was deadly and getting caught would surely mean their execution.

The captain accepted the offer with that crazy look in his eyes. Like he'd already figured something out, something that made John uncomfortable. It didn't take long for John to put the pieces together, but he turned a blind eye.

He hated RAM and didn't care if they paid the price for how they believed. Also, he was eating and lived in relatively safe housing at the Buffalo Coast Guard Station. He considered it only relatively safe because the soldiers guarding the place were somewhat incompetent. And the other survivors living at the station were an unsavory bunch. But he was eating regular meals!

At the three-minute mark, Captain Riggins turned the

tug starboard, then hard to port aligning with the beach where they would deliver the cargo. He accelerated and when the tug was under a mile from shore, he cut power to the engines. The sudden deceleration caused the cargo to shift forward, opening the cargo doors. When the modified barge made contact with sand and rock, he initiated a full reverse.

The barge tilted slightly forward, dumping a portion of its cargo about five hundred yards from the shore. He hit the hydraulic motor that started tilting the cargo deck towards the shore, causing his cargo to spill freely into Lake Eire. The stench overwhelmed his senses and forced his eyes to tear, blurring his vision so badly he couldn't see the front of the barge.

But he didn't need visual confirmation to know what was happening. Thousands of the dead spilled into the water to be carried to shore by the currents. The water churned red under his tug's propellers as the powerful motors propelled the tug away from the ghastly scene.

The dead filled the beach, bumping and slamming into each other like some sick mosh-pit. Those that fell to the sandy earth were immediately ground to a bloody pulp. The stench was indescribable as was the noise coming from the beach. Those raspy wet groans, which they'd just recently started making, sent chills down his spine.

Some undead moved to the roadway and into the city, splitting in two directions. One group shambled east; the other was forced to the west by natural and manmade barriers. They trampled everything in their path as they churned up the earth on the way to the road. Hundreds of them had made it to the roadway and beyond, searching for their next meal.

As he watched the grotesque undulating mass of dead flesh, the captain figured this would be the last trip to this area for his vessel. With twenty or more barges just like this one heading to the shoreline today, the bodies in the water would soon cause problems for the vessels' props and motors.

He wondered aloud where his next haul would take him. No doubt it would be another RAM-held city, and he couldn't have been happier about it.

CHAPTER 21:
THEY NEVER CHANGE

TWO WEEKS EARLIER

The senator from NY removed his reading glasses perched on the tip of his nose as he peered, in his pompous manner, at the man dressed in black fatigues.

"I told you, your gun is to stay in the hall, Williams," he said in his usual condescending, self-righteous tone.

"And I told you, Senator, until you idiots find a cure for this thing; I'll always have, at the very least, two guns with me." His tenor was much harder than the Senator's and dripped with contempt. "You see, I don't have a security detail. I *am* the security detail."

Williams couldn't stand politicians, and this one was a perfect example why. Instead of working to fix things, he was doing what politicians did best: handing it off to someone else and using it to gain power. Never mind his actions would kill more innocent people. All that mattered to the Senator was power.

The Senator waved off his comments. "Have your men been able to pull the RAM troops off the shoreline?"

Williams adjusted his position before responding. "If by men you mean the boys we sent to certain death to run shoot and scoots in RAM-held areas, the boys with no military training, who'd never even seen a gun until we put one in their hands? Then yes. We have INTEL that, for now, it seems to be working. Although they're having a difficult time telling the difference between a soldier and well-armed civilians. They've been shooting at both indiscriminately, but not hitting anything. They haven't reported a single hit on either group. God help them if they get into a firefight. They won't last ten minutes."

The Senator leaned back in his plush leather chair, the one he'd had Williams' men transport to this location at the Buffalo Coast Guard Station. The chair that caused his men to leave valuable supplies behind to make room for. He promised himself that he would shove it up the Senator's ass when this was over.

"We don't like guns or the people that use them, Mr. Williams. You're a necessary evil, at best, but more like lackeys that keep the people that run this country safe. Those boys, as you call them, are better served with minimal exposure to those things. Lest they become a servant, not unlike yourself. They are serving a greater good, taking back what is ours. To reclaim the resources which rightfully belong to BSU."

Williams' blood boiled as he used every muscle in his body to remain seated and not snap the Senator's neck. He leaned across the desk and noticed a twitch of anxiety from the Senator as he did so.

He said, in as calm a voice as he could muster, "Speaking

of resources, why are we burning them on this project? We have barely any resources left, and the last pockets of our citizens are being overrun. We have lost this fight and need to save who we can and regroup."

The Senator smugly replied, "Well, you just answered your own question."

Williams grimaced, understanding he meant that the people left alive in BSU could count only on being left to fend for themselves. That the endgame, for BSU leaders, was to take what others had built and fought to hold on to and make it theirs. To move directly into the power structure and take it over.

He spoke in a flat tone, leaving no room for question or debate. "Know this; I will tear a piece of your body off for every boy that dies during this mission. When I run out of appendages, I'm going to tear your throat out. Remember, the lackey who's standing guard outside your door reports to me."

With that he stood and walked out. The Senator started to babble something about soldier boy doing his job, but he blocked him out and continued walking.

After the door slammed, the Senator mumbled a question to himself. "What did you do, Mr. Kim? It wasn't supposed to be this bad."

CHAPTER 22:
THE INVITATION

About a quarter mile from our community, the Jeep started to slip in and out of gear. A problem the dealership said didn't exist until after my warranty ran out. I knew it would happen eventually, but not during the end of the world when I had no one to call and berate.

Darline realized what was happening and turned to look out the window to avoid eye contact. The Jeep always put me in a bad mood. I've been known to rant for hours about how ten different mechanics worked on it and not one of them could fix it. Or even *recreate* the symptoms. If someone ever says that to me again, my head WILL explode.

Lisa started to ask what was happening when Darline held up a hand. "Not now, Lisa, not now." Sensing it was a deeper issue, Lisa let it go.

She sat back in her seat and looked to be reciting a quick prayer... best idea she'd had all day!

The Jeep limped to the community and stopped moving about thirty feet from the gate. Not a big issue on most days. But with several hundred pounds of supplies in the back that now needed to be transferred to another vehicle, then into our community, it became a big deal. I wasn't in the mood for any of it!

Dillan walked over to meet us. Looking at my bright red face, he asked, "What's the matter?"

I let him know that the Jeep had finally died on me. I sat in the driver seat, both hands on the wheel, squeezing it until my knuckles turned white, looking straight ahead. He made an *Oh boy* face and walked past me to Stone and Kit. He told them how to access the gate and that our quarantine rules, for new arrivals, would have them segregated for seventy-two hours.

I heard him give the direction to Stone and called out to Dillan with a question. "What about Andy, how do we keep them separated?"

Dillan, not wanting to get too close to me because of the current situation with my Jeep, yelled his response to me. "We sectioned three houses off for quarantine so they won't come into contact with each other."

I got out and ran over to my brother as he exited his SUV, I wrapped him in a tight hug. It was sinking in how close I had come to losing him and I just needed a minute with him.

When we broke apart, he looked at me and said, "Well, I'd love to help you with that Jeep of yours, but I need to get into quarantine." A smile was curling the corners of his mouth when he continued, "The chances of you finding someone to fix that thing are nil now that the world has ended. And I think I told you to trade it in about four months ago, yep, I did."

I suddenly didn't like him anymore. "Go to your quarantine. I'll be asking them not to feed you for the next three days." It was a hollow threat, but the best I could do. He walked away laughing and got into his SUV and pulled through the gate.

Lisa and Darline had joined Stone and Kit. They cleared their bite check, helped get Stone and Kit settled, and then headed home, leaving me to unload the supplies with Dillan.

It took about fifteen minutes to unpack and move the Jeep off the road. My mood lightened after I realized I might not find a mechanic, but I shouldn't have a problem finding a new SUV. With dozens of abandoned cars and SUVs I'd have my pick. I saw a Tahoe in my future. I put it on my list of things to get done in the morning.

While unloading, I asked Dillan if the Black Hawk had landed in our community or if he had seen any activity related to it in the area.

"It passed overhead, slowed down while passing over, and then headed directly to the area around the drugstore. After that, we lost visuals on them. They didn't hang around long."

As long as no one was shooting, I'd call it a good thing.

He mentioned that the tower guards had reported a sharp uptick in the amount of the things over the last two days. I told him we now called them UCs. He liked it.

His next statement made little sense at first. "Otto, the guards also reported that a number of the UCs were wearing New York gear."

I asked, "What do you mean by *gear*?"

He said, "Hats from Buffalo on several and a group of about eight that had Niagara Falls shirts on."

I said, "It might be nothing. Just some people taking vacations at a terrible time."

With a slight dip in his voice, he said, "Otto, we also had a group with Yankees shirts on."

That got my attention. There was not a chance someone in RAM would get caught wearing a Yankees shirt.

People just didn't wear them in RAM. Even when they were in town for a game, you simply didn't see them. The people of RAM can forgive a lot of transgressions, but Yankees baseball isn't one of them.

I asked, "How many more UCs are they seeing?"

Dillan was quick to respond, "On average, about ten percent more. They seem to be coming from the northeast. We spotted the ones we're talking about roughly two miles away from us."

I realized that Dillan was taking his position one hundred percent seriously and performing it meticulously. He'd realized that initiating a daily count of the UCs would give us a base from which to determine if the numbers were growing. Subsequently, we could use that information to make security changes like sending out patrols to thin them out or bolster the guards at our walls.

I asked him, "How many living are you seeing?"

His response was encouraging. "We think we've identified several smaller communities like ours. And, we've been seeing about ten to twenty individuals or small groups a day. We're not sure if they're repeats or new each day. But it's been steady."

He told me that after the drugstore supply run, he'd gotten to work organizing teams to conduct supply runs throughout the week. Possibly several a day. It was a *first-pass* list of volunteers, but he said he had no problem getting people to step up.

When we stopped talking, I reported to have Bill do my bite screening. Honestly, I was so tired at this point I could have been covered in bites and wouldn't have known it. After the checkout and some ball busting from Bill, I headed home.

During my walk I couldn't escape the thought... *this isn't how I thought the end of the world would be.*

I got home, showered, walked to our bedroom, and that's the last thing I remember. By the time I crawled into bed, my body was running on fumes. Remember I'm in good shape but I'm still fiftyish, and every part of me hurt. I work out, but not zombie-apocalypse workout. The last couple of days were a blur of violence and death. I needed to rest before it overtook my mind and my body.

Morning arrived with an incredible amount of clatter from outside the gate and from overhead. It sounded like the entire RAM military had arrived to conduct full-scale war-games. Unannounced war-games to be exact.

It impressed me the way Dillan's group handled the military's arrival at our community. This kid had the group running like a machine. I felt safe with him and his team on watch. They fell into assigned defensive positions, some obvious and some not. Now, don't get me wrong. We didn't stand a chance against the well-armed military unit at our gate. But we would hurt them if it turned into a fight.

I tossed cotton shorts and a tee-shirt on and headed for the door, resembling a drunk who had just gotten off a bar stool and realized he was late for work. I grabbed my radio and gun belt on the way out the door. The gun belt added the finishing touch to my already unruly appearance.

I radioed Dillan while I did a run-hop thing on the way to the gate. He got back to me to tell me he was also on his way. Then he added that Bill told him someone named Willis, Sergeant Willis, had asked for me.

Willis, my main military man, was holding true to his word and stopping by about the military equipment program he'd told me about. I felt like a kid on Christmas morning. Albeit, a kid that walked with a limp because everything on his body hurt. A kid that had to do a run-hop walk to the gate because even his toenails ached. *This apocalypse had better wrap up in the next couple weeks because I was wearing out fast.*

Willis waited at the gate with his trademark smile on overdrive. With the relaxed posture he and his men had taken, I figured they were trying to keep tensions low while we made introductions. However, I was sure the Bradleys that sat facing our community stood ready to unleash hellfire if needed. The action showed he was well-aware of how jumpy we'd all become, and hinted that he had probably run into more than one situation with people like us.

Remember, we are all heavily armed these days and guns plus jumpy can lead to bad things happening.

The Black Hawk had disappeared behind a tree-line about three blocks away. Undoubtedly ready to be called into service at a moment's notice.

"Sergeant Willis, you woke me up, good sir," I said with a half-smile and awful morning breath.

He looked me over while shaking his head as if saying *Well, the drunk guy's late for work.*

"Otto, do you need a minute or two, maybe twenty, to pull yourself together?"

I started to blurt out a smartass answer, but he was right. I looked like hell and I needed coffee! "I do, and you woke me up." With that I turned and walked home to pull myself together.

On my way home, I saw Randy on course to intercept me. I figured he'd be unhappy about me going to get my brother without him. And, it appeared, I was about to find out how unhappy, but he just kept glaring at me as he passed me. No stop, no nod, no assault. I wanted to ask him to meet up with me and Willis, but he just kept walking.

I think I was a little offended, maybe even hurt, that he

didn't say a word. He didn't even ask me about the mission to save my brother. So I made a hard stop and asked, "What?"

He hadn't stopped staring at me. "I'm headed to talk to your brother, make sure he's *comfortable*. He was nice enough to let me know he and Kit are safe. You, on the other hand, you look like hell, and I don't think I care how you feel." And that was it. He kept walking. At one point he walked backwards so he could keep glaring at me. Then, he about-faced and headed for my brothers' temporary housing. I can't be sure, but he may have flipped me off while turning around.

It's good to see Randy hadn't allowed the end of the world to change him.

A shower and two cups of coffee later and I headed out to meet Willis, with other members of the community in tow. During the time I was cleaning up, he had made nice with Dillan, cutting down on the tension at the gate.

Willis had also supplied us with an M939 five-ton truck full of MREs. The MREs were a Godsend that would help keep this community alive through the coming months. I'd been praying it would only be months. We didn't get to keep the truck, but the food compensated for that.

Two additional M939 trucks remained outside the gate under heavy guard. Dillan had allowed all other troops and vehicles to enter the community, so whatever was in the trucks was important. It appeared we didn't meet the level of trust needed to get close to them. Well, now I *needed* to know what was in the damn trucks.

Willis briefed us on what was happening in the world. He told us it had become a worldwide extinction level event, one that we may never bounce back from. RAM was holding its own, but we had a precarious grip on things.

He informed us that power would become more sporadic in the coming weeks as they tried to get their arms around the thirty-five nuclear power plants inside RAM's borders.

That slice of crap-news ripped my attention away from the trucks and to thinking about living another day. "What do you mean, *get our arms around them*?" I asked, unable to mask the urgency in my voice. "Isn't that something our arms should've been glued to?"

We have two nuclear plants in Ohio with a couple in other states close to our borders. If they went China-syndrome on us, we could kiss the tiny slices of our lives that we had salvaged goodbye. The apocalypse was really becoming a pain-in-my-ass.

Willis noticed he'd struck a nerve, so he made clear what he was talking about. "Nationwide, we've been clearing them of any UC infestations then determining if we can take them offline until we can get the appropriate teams assigned to them. They're running on failsafe systems and seem to be in good order. But it's too dangerous to let them run on chance. Three of them remained functional while manned by the original operators. We moved the families of the entire operating team to the facilities and locked them down. Several others have been secured by our people. We took them offline and assigned crews to bring them back online in the next couple of weeks. The ones in BSU are unknowns at this point because we can't get anyone in the BSU to pick up a phone, radio, or carrier pigeon for that matter. The pot's boiling over with no one minding the kitchen."

After he finished, we fixed him with unblinking eyes. It was safe to say some of us were in shock. We were visualizing our own destruction – being cooked alive by radiation.

He broke our stupor by telling us that the uptick in UC activity they'd seen didn't add up. The shoot and scoots (SAS) seem to be related to the increase of UC. Furthermore, the SAS always happened south of Lake Erie, within three miles of the shoreline, five to six miles east and west of each other. It was a consistent pattern. When you marked each SAS on a map, it formed a perfect fan pattern from Edgewater Beach out to neighboring cities. The UC activity picked up after a SAS occurred. It was like clockwork.

We asked him about the safe zones that some of our people had migrated to. He said they were crowded, not always comfortable, but safe. The food and water distribution centers were a different story. They sent extra troops to some of them because of the violence that was erupting. It spiked after throngs of people, with no RAM-ID, showed up trying to move to the front of the lines.

People were beaten, some killed, for the meager supplies received from the distribution center.

It was just the way I'd thought it would be. I was confident we'd made the right choice in avoiding the distribution centers and safe zones. Hopefully, Dillan would soon get our scavenging teams together and yield enough to hold us through the coming winter.

Willis asked for a minute alone with me to review some other issues. We took a walk around the community to check out the progress the residents had made in fortifying our home.

We put about fifty yards between us and the group when I asked, "What's on your mind, Willis?"

He pulled to a slow stop and said, "I'm assuming you were reading between the lines when I talked about the power plants. I could see the wheels turning in your head while I spoke." He paused for a second before continuing. "Otto, we're getting stretched thin. We're running non-stop out of Hopkins shoring up the breach in the Illinois/Indiana border Entry Point. It's eating up resources." His obvious concern about the situation made me anxious.

"The military is still running patrols along the border wall, more to the west, engaging more and more UC and civilians. Our Entry Points are swamped with refugees and UC. We've had some breaches but overall we're holding." He noticed the breach statement got my attention. "Otto," he continued, "there's nothing to worry about, yet, but we need to get it under control."

I had a suspicion I knew what was coming. We weren't getting military support; we were going to *be* military support.

"We suspect the SAS activity is a distraction to spread us even thinner and take advantage of the gaps. The crowds that gather at the west wall sometimes appear like they're being dropped off by the bus load. And we have some INTEL that the increased activity in this area is not a natural occurrence."

I interrupted him when he said that last part. "Willis, our guys spotted some out-of-place UC groups yesterday."

Willis cut in. "What do you mean *out-of-place*?"

"Well, they were wearing a lot of New York gear. But it was the group wearing Yankees shirts that didn't add up."

Willis went rigid. "Where did you spot them?" he asked while grabbing his radio. I told him Dillan had the information. I grabbed my walkie and asked him to join us.

Dillan caught up with us a few minutes later. He told Willis what they'd been seeing and the general location of the sightings. Willis stepped away and was speaking into his radio when we heard the Black Hawk fire up. It was airborne a minute after, heading in the direction Dillan had identified. I kept thinking, *This isn't a good sign.*

Willis asked Dillan to give us a second and walked back to me. "Otto, the soft sell is over. We need to grab a few of your best. Get them, and you, trained to help shore up our defenses by providing force in less lethal situations."

I looked at him quizzically. "Willis, that's not much of an invitation. Also, I don't recall seeing or hearing about a declaration of war that triggered a draft or militia formation. You have hundreds if not thousands of citizens living in the safe zones, why not use them?"

I could tell Willis was worn out. His trademark smile had vanished as had the look of the young man he was. What stood before me was a battle-hardened warrior who'd been forced to kill the citizens he'd sworn an oath to protect. To fire upon civilians trying to breach the security of his home. They might not be from RAM, but they were civilians nonetheless. He was taking orders from people that had no idea what he and his men had witnessed in the streets of his home country. And now, he was being forced to ask citizens for help. To ask citizens to risk their lives because he'd failed at his sworn duty.

You could see the physical effort employed by Willis to maintain his composure after my remarks about the draft and safe zones. He closed his eyes for a long minute. When he opened them, they locked on mine and he told me exactly why our community had received the invitation.

"Otto, we've been thinking about this for a while, even before we met at Hopkins. We've been utilizing the population at the safe zones for many jobs. But remember, they came to the zones to seek safety, not to put themselves in harm's way. They've been effective at defending the fence from the few UC build-ups that we've had. Nevertheless, they aren't interested in taking it further than that. Your community, and ones like it, are full of people who are ready to fight to keep what's yours while keeping your community safe. We need you to help us take this country back. You have the fighting spirit born into people, not learned, and we need that spirit. We need that fighting spirit, but most of all, Otto, we just need some help."

Well shit, I didn't expect the speech to end with that little gut punch. One never expects a soldier, a battle-hardened soldier at that, to need help let alone ask for help. I gave it some thought and told him I would talk to the community. But I needed all the information on the scope of the support they were asking for. We'd need to know about the tools they'd supply, and the assurance that our community would stay an independent entity. Relief spread over his face, and the tension left his body. He looked at me with his trademark smile back and said one word, "Deal."

"So," I started, "what's in the trucks?"

Willis gave a slight nod and chuckled. "It's been killing you not knowing, hasn't it?"

He wore a big dorky grin, but he was one hundred percent correct – it was killing me not knowing what was waiting outside of our gates.

"What's in the trucks?" I asked again.

Willis said, "Talk to your community and, depending on the outcome, we can talk about what's in the trucks." He had me and he knew it.

"Whatever," I shot back and walked away in a huff.

CHAPTER 23:
AND THE YEAS HAVE IT??

I talked to Pat and Darline about the invitation from Willis and the challenges our military faced. Both had apprehensions about what it ultimately meant for our community. But they agreed that if it were truly a voluntary service, no one could prevent our people from joining the effort. We weren't captors or dictators; our community was free to do as they wished.

We pulled a larger group together to see what they thought, comprised of Al, Dillan, Randy, who still wasn't talking to me, Bill, and Will. I had talked to Stone and Andy via radio from their quarantine and both wanted in. But I needed to hear all the details before fully committing to them.

When I talked to Andy, he said he wasn't feeling himself, not bad or sick or dead, just not *right*. He imposed an open-ended quarantine on himself. The conversation concerned me. We didn't have an adequate amount of information about the virus. Had it mutated again? Why was he sick but not turning into a UC? Thank God he was smart enough to recognize that and keep himself locked down. The paramedic couple had started giving him a mixture of antiviral and antibiotics a few days before, so fingers crossed the drugs helped.

Everyone I talked to agreed. We should proceed by presenting the offer to the entire community, letting them decide how to act on the invitation. So we pulled them all together, with Willis and a couple of his men joining us to review the details of the invitation. We set up a meeting area in the cul-de-sac at the end of my street.

The faces looked familiar but somehow different. Many looked hard, as if this event had steeled them, and they were ready to exact some revenge on the virus. Others just looked exhausted, wanting to travel back in time. Back to life before the virus but knowing it was gone forever.

I started by giving them a summary of what was happening and what the military wanted. They shifted and mumbled amongst themselves after I explained the invitation and why they had picked our community. At that point I turned it over to Willis.

He got up and put it as plainly as possible. They needed us to reduce the load on the military. We would make supply runs, perform search and rescue, and do reconnaissance. Maybe even thin out UC-infested areas threatening to overrun communities like ours.

They would train us for two weeks. The training would include weapons training. We found that amusing until Willis clarified it would be on weapons we'd never used. My head spun in his direction and I blurted out, "What's in the trucks, Willis?"

He smiled and nodded. "Let's open the *floor* for volunteers, then we can talk about it."

The mention of military weapons got the crowd a little more animated. Turns out Randy and me aren't the only gun nuts in the neighborhood.

The rules were simple. We weren't joining or committing to the military long term. The military would provide support in the form of weapons, ammunition, training, logistical support, mission intelligence, and extraction support should something go wrong. The community would remain autonomous, our own little nation so to speak.

He admitted it would be confusing for everyone initially, but with time it should work itself out. Willis finished with the same easygoing approach with which he had started his presentation. He recognized he had no reason to *sell* the idea. The military was asking us to do something extraordinarily dangerous. More dangerous than the danger we faced just trying to survive. We wanted in or we didn't, so no hard sell tactics were needed.

As he spoke, I looked at the families that comprised our community. Single moms like Tesha. The young adults like Andros Galanos who at nineteen was now the parent figure for his three younger siblings. I realized something had to be done to stop some of them from volunteering for the Military Support Teams (MSTs), as Willis had named them. We were becoming a real community. If we wanted to continue building it, we needed vital parts to be dedicated solely to its success.

When Willis wrapped up, I quickly interjected before anyone volunteered. I told them the military also put some limitations on who could volunteer.

Willis had a surprised look on his face and moved in closer to me. He leaned in and asked, "Um, Otto, what're you up to?"

"Willis, just give me a minute, and you'll understand. You'll also realize I needed to do it."

Willis moved back a step, surrendering the floor to me, well the grassy spot that is.

The group had grown a little restless but calmed down when I started to speak. "Not unlike when the U.S. military was using the draft, we will exclude certain members of our community from volunteering."

My statement set off some anxiety and what sounded like a bit of anger in the crowd. So, being me, I immediately blamed the military and continued, "Not my rules, Willis and his Command set the ground rules for the MSTs." I tried to take some heat off Willis, who was now facing me with a look of exasperation on his face, by saying, "And I agree with him."

It was at this point that I realized I'm more unpopular than I thought. And I probably should've taken time to get to know my neighbors. The crowd's reaction was a little abrasive with someone shouting, "Oh, thank you, Mr. Hammer, I feel much better now that you agree with the military." Followed by, "Why should I care if you agree with them?" I think I recognized Randy as the owner of that last comment. His smug smile, as he stood behind the crowd, let me know he was both enjoying this and involved in the heckling. Man, that guy can hold a grudge.

Pat noticed me squirming under the pressure and walked over to join me. "What are you getting at, Otto?" she asked quietly enough so the crowd wouldn't hear.

"Nothing that should cause the meanness I'm seeing; it's actually a very thoughtful move on my part."

Pat rolled her eyes at my self-praising and asked everyone to give me a minute.

The crowd obviously liked her better than me, because they responded to her request instantly.

"Okay," I started, "the persons falling under the following statuses cannot volunteer because of your importance to the community overall. Parents and guardians, single or otherwise, of children under the age of eighteen. Persons under eighteen, persons already assigned to or performing a vital function including security." I detected Dillan's bristle but kept speaking. "Only one member of a family unit living in the same house with other qualified persons. Or, persons with physical limitations preventing them from performing at the military's prescribed levels for the MSTs."

With that, I dismissed myself. I joined Willis and Randy as we broke from the crowd now being directed to consider the offer to join MST1. Willis asked me why I had used the military as an excuse to exclude certain people.

"Knowing we can't stop anyone in the community from volunteering. And that they're free to do as they please because we're not a prison camp. I needed to come up with something to keep some of them safe. In turn, keeping the community safe. So, I used the military, which we still respect in RAM, as my cover. Enough children have been orphaned already and we need to make sure we don't orphan more."

Willis and Randy looked shocked I was smart enough to think those rules through on the fly. I'm getting the impression that people really don't think highly of me.

I broke the awkward staring contest by asking, "Willis, what's in the trucks? I held up my part of the bargain, so let's go to the trucks."

Randy leaned close to Willis and whispered something that made the sergeant crack a crooked, evil little smile. It became clear Willis knew he could have some fun with me.

"So, Otto, you need to know what's in the trucks?" Willis started when I cut him off.

"Randy, you need to work on your anger issues and stop being so vindictive. You weren't asked to go because we'd been running full throttle for, what, two or three days? You were sleeping when Darline called you and we left it at that."

Unfazed, Randy again leaned into Willis and whispered. Then Willis said, "Randy isn't talking to you."

Shaking my head, I started walking to the trucks.

I said, loud enough for them to hear, "I'm dealing with children."

We moved the trucks inside the gate because some UC shambled on scene and we wanted to avoid drawing more. They parked by the quarantine houses because the community had erected a fence around the three homes. This enabled them to better control access to the trucks. The fenced area left enough room for the big M939s to park perpendicular to the houses, giving them thirty feet between their front doors and the trucks.

As I approached the quarantine area, I was again impressed with how quickly this community had pulled together to defend itself. The fencing alone was impressive and had gone up in the first days after the virus accelerated its spread across the world. We were now almost four weeks into this mess and had already become a haven for survivors.

I walked to the gate and one of the gate guards let me in. The fence surrounding the quarantine area was about six feet high. It looked like fencing panels that were bolted or spiked to the ground. It had two additional feet of barbed wire at the top and a line of large boulders along its outside base. If you cleared the fence, you would assuredly break an ankle when you landed.

When the guard opened the gate, I turned to Randy and Willis only to find they had fallen about thirty feet behind. Apparently, I had walked off in a huff after Willis and Randy teamed up. I really hope it didn't look like I was stomping my feet when I left them in the cul-de-sac. I may have been, but I really didn't want them to know that they'd gotten to me.

Willis and Randy caught up quickly enough, and we entered the gate and proceeded to the first M939. Willis turned to me and, with a deadpan expression, asked, "Otto, are you sure you're ready for this? Ready to behold the wonderment that awaits you on the other side of the canvas enclosure?" Randy started to laugh, and I almost stomped off again.

"Sergeant Willis, please open this truck before my head explodes."

Willis gave a slight smile with a curt nod and opened the back of the first M939. I expected a small arsenal. I wanted mortars, Javelin Weapons Systems, stacks of M4s, rows of M240s and M249s and mountains of ammunition for all of them.

What I found was a perfect example of reality not meeting expectations. Actually, I felt like a little kid that ran downstairs on Christmas morning and found someone had stolen everything from under the tree.

The truck was loaded with supplies I'm confident people would consider useful or even necessary for survival. It contained several large military medical kits. I'm talking full medical kits, not a first aid kit with forty bandages and sting-relief spray. It also contained several other smaller mobile kits. I saw radios, alternative power sources like solar and small wind turbines, and a mix of black and digi-cam

ACUs. Not one thing that shot bullets or blew stuff up.

I stared blankly at Willis, who really didn't seem to understand the disappointment written all over my face. Randy, for his part, was trying so hard to not laugh at me he was turning red.

"Willis, I'm going to need more. More than some ACUs and medical kits. You're asking this community to support the military by putting themselves in danger of being killed and or eaten."

Moreover, I wanted to tinker with some of the finest weapons the military had to offer, not play dress up!

"Okay, not quite the reaction I expected, so let's move on," Willis said as he turned to his right and headed for the next truck. I glanced at the middle quarantine house and could see my brother looking out of a second-story window. When we made eye contact, he made a *Well, what's in the truck* gesture. I responded with a thumbs down.

My reaction came from the fact that nothing the truck held went BANG. I completely overlooked the life-saving items they had given us. I might need to accept that I'm a jerk.

When he finished revelling in my anguish. I noticed Randy also looked wholly dejected by the contents of the truck. He walked up behind us as we stood at the gate of the second truck and put his hand on my shoulder. I glanced back at him and found him staring, stoically, at the truck. The act of solidarity might seem a bit dramatic, but honestly, it helped ease the disappointment.

Willis still looked befuddled by my reaction and pulled the canvas back on truck number two. It was like the celestial sky parted. Warm light seemed to bathe our faces as a cool breeze fluffed our hair. I could hear angels in the background singing *ahhhhhh* in the most beautiful tone to have ever filled my ears.

I beheld the contents of the truck. It was nearly the best moment of my life. This was what I'd been hoping for. The mother-lode. Every man, woman, and child's dream, a truck full of guns. I looked back at Randy, and I believe he was wiping a tear away from his eye. He looked at me and embraced me in a man hug to beat all man hugs. Man hug: right hand gripping the other man's in a handshake placed between the two of you while slapping the other man's back with your free hand. It's a man thing.

I peeked around the truck, giving Stone double thumbs up and sending him into gyrations of man joy. In that moment, we forgot all that was bad and breathed in the aroma of gun oil and cleaning solvent. The sight of two dozen M4s, four M249s, one M107 LRSR (long range sniper rifle), two M110 Sniper Systems, and crates and crates of ammunition made it all better!

I turned to Willis and moved to hug him. Willis would have none of it and moved hard to the right and climbed into the truck. He became deadly serious while surveying the truck. Glancing back at me and Randy, he said, "Otto, Randy, don't make me regret this. It wasn't easy to get Command to part with these items. If you two go sideways, it'll be all our asses on the line. Got it?"

I realized things must be getting really bad for this to happen. The military wasn't in the habit of loaning weaponry to civilians, especially during times of war or zombie apocalypses.

I looked at him and said, "I understand the chance you're taking and the same goes for us. You need to recognize that we are one hundred percent committed to living and to beating this... this, whatever it is. We'll work with you, not for you, but with you. You can trust us."

While Randy jumped into the bed of the truck and headed to the M107s, Willis reached down and offered me a hand up. He gave me a long stare and nodded his head as if to say *Okay, I trust you.*

He said, "Get the community leaders together and make sure to include Dillan. We'll unload the trucks because the training starts today." That statement created a pit in my stomach. He followed up with, "You realize not all of this is for your group, right? You're the first group to test, not the only group. We have a real shit storm swirling around the world and must distribute the weaponry effectively."

Son of a b—! It WAS too good to be true! I looked back at Randy who dropped one of the ammo crates after hearing the news. He may have wiped another tear from his eye, and I think I heard him whimper ever so softly... so sad. Then, going for the kill, Willis added, "And your group gets one less M4, because, Mr. Otto, seems like you found a stash of them."

Too sad to fight back, the best I could come up with was, "Fine, whatever, blah blah blah." I literally said the blahs part. Not my finest moment.

CHAPTER 24:
LEARNING HOW TO FIGHT

We ended up with about twenty volunteers, but only seven that qualified per the rules I'd made up. Of the seven, one sat in quarantine, still not feeling one hundred percent. Andy's situation was becoming critical, and we would need to determine if it was the scratch or something else. Whatever it was, he was not getting better.

So the team consisted of me, Randy, Stone, Jax, Lisa, and Will. Turned out Will was former military so he assumed command of one of the three-person teams. I felt a sense of relief that Will would be leading a team. I was already uncomfortable with being an ad hoc leader of the community. So the notion of leading a group of six in the hostile environment outside our fence turned my stomach. Why three people sounded better than six? I can't say, it just did. Maybe because my team consisted of me, Stone, and Randy. I trusted them and they understood me. More importantly they knew when to ignore me. It would probably keep them alive.

Dillan and a few of the gate and security guards helped unload the trucks. It thrilled the paramedic couple, who had assumed the roles of community doctors, to see the first truck's contents. They had them moved to one of the larger, uninhabited homes and set up a clinic of sorts. I'll need to learn their names. Pat was right about me.

I stopped and thought, *We are turning into a real community. We have a chance at living through this nightmare.* You could see the pride taking root in the people that stayed. *We can do this!*

Willis wasn't kidding. After emptying the trucks, he pulled us together to start our training. He informed us we'd be skipping the Boot Camp portion because we needed to get up and running ASAP. The urgency led me to believe that we would roll out directly after we finished our training.

We built a small range on the south side of the community. It faced into some abandoned homes immediately outside the fence. We pulled a portion of fencing free so we didn't obliterate it while we practiced. Then our training officially started, with a BANG.

Over the course of the next two weeks, we learned the intimate details of every weapon in our arsenal. We spent one full day on proper mag swapping. Another day on how to control our rifles when in full-auto. We learned that selecting full auto on the M4A1 or the three-shot burst on the M4 made them difficult to control. Accuracy dropped to crowd suppression levels, only useful for living beings that shot back. Or when employing the strategy of disabling large throngs of UCs to create chokepoints or roadblocks and buying ourselves time to retreat. Past that, full auto was a hazard.

Stone had joined us a day after we started training and decided he would stick with his favorite gun. He chose his Tavor X95 Bullpup for the close-up stuff. The guy was dead nuts with it, and it became an extension of his body during our training.

The part of the training that I thought would be the most fun – shooting military weapons – fell kind of flat. Don't get me wrong. The M249 is without a doubt an adrenaline rush the likes of which I've never had. But I already had the M4 from Westley's house. So, *meh* was what came to mind.

We covered basic first aid and training on flash bangs. No grenades. Willis claimed he didn't trust me. Not the rest of the team, just me. I took it personally. They introduced us to night vision goggles and the military version of plate-carriers and ACUs. The Wideband Handheld Radio was another story. None of us got the hang of it so we kept our radios and would use the Wide Band in case of emergency. Considering they had only issued one, emergency contact with the military was pretty much all it was good for.

However, they focused heavily on clearing houses, stressing that we needed to avoid shooting one another. Thanks, Captain Obvious. We drilled houses for a full week. Day after day, hour after hour, Willis and his men ran us through the drills. We changed houses for every drill. We cleared every style of home we could in our community. It was hard, hot, and mentally draining, but we got it down and started to become effective teams.

Each night Darline was subjected to stories about my day. And, every story was about clearing houses. She finally told me that unless I did something new, she didn't want to hear about it. She was busy helping Pat run the day to day and began working the gate, part-time, with Dillan. Then she told me she didn't have the energy to listen to me *drone* on. She's kinda mean that way.

The final day of training came with a surprise: We got a Humvee assigned to us. Now, to be precise, it looked like a military surplus vehicle, but it ran and would hold all of us. I did, of course, ask Willis, "Why no APV or Bradley?"

"Because we need to be able to stop you if you go rogue, Otto."

He had a point.

We drove that thing for hours upon hours. We drove it over hills and stumps, hauled felled trees out of our way using the winch, and then created a muddy field and learned how to pull ourselves out with the winch. We quickly became a nuisance to the community. Eventually, Pat shut us down. She stood in the middle of the street when we started down her street for the fifth or sixth time.

Pat put up her hand and walked to the Humvee. She leaned in and said, "We're getting ready to take a vote to have all of you removed from the community. So, unless you want to sleep outside the fence in your new little toy, you'll be shutting it down."

I told you before, Pat's tough as nails and her delivery

left no doubt that we had pushed her to the edge. We looked at her like a bunch of kids that got busted coming home past curfew. It would have been comical if we hadn't been so intimidated by her.

"Sorry, Pat, we'll wrap it up now," I said. I backed the Humvee away from her while we all stared at her waiting for her to get really mad. We lucked out and escaped the angry-Pat-zone before she started throwing punches and drove back to the impromptu training area.

Stone, who had never met Pat, leaned between the front seats and asked, "What was that? She scared the crap out of me."

The rest of us answered "Pat." Enough said.

CHAPTER 25: 0600

After we wrapped up for the day, we met with Lewis. He'd stayed behind while Willis moved on to train the next MST.

He said, "Will, you and your team need to meet me at 0600 tomorrow. We have a situation by Entry Point One that needs your attention."

"Entry Point One? We thought we'd deploy close to home, supporting the local area."

Lewis, who's about twenty-two, six foot even, and built like an athlete, paused. It looked like he was reminding himself that we weren't in the military and needed to be handled differently.

He said in a forced calm voice, "Will, I'll see you at 0600 tomorrow to go over the mission details." With that, he headed back to the Mobile Shelter System they occupied in our community during our training.

Darline wasn't happy when I told her about the distance and the team being nearly impossible to contact during the mission. But we understood what it meant to be on an MST. We could help turn this around, stop the spiral the country was in.

"Hazelton, West Virginia? That's a three-and-a-half-hour trip, if all the freeways are passable."

Will wasn't happy about the distance the night before and he wasn't happy at 0600. He pointed out that our training had only been two weeks with none of it focusing on sleep deprivation, managing exhaustion, or night fighting. All which was possible with a three-hour ride before we even reached our target. After he finished, and sensing he wasn't getting anywhere, he asked, "What's the mission-objective?"

Lewis had been quiet through Will's entire diatribe. And it looked like Will finished just in time because beads of sweat had formed on Lewis' forehead and he looked to be in a foul mood.

"Okay, if there's nothing further, I'll continue the briefing." Lewis paused, like he was waiting for someone else to interrupt him. When it didn't happen, he continued. "Actually, Hazelton is your first stop. We have a brigade-sized force in the area which has commandeered the prisons. The virus wreaked havoc on the inmate population, so we cleared out the infected and took over the buildings. We also have ample firepower at Entry Point One. You'll stop in Hazelton, refuel, eat, and whatever else you need to do. After which you'll head to the Tactical Operations Center where you'll receive further instruction."

He paused for a minute and grabbed a box that held what looked like security cards. The kind you would use in an office building to unlock doors or gain access to certain areas of the complex. The box also had a large manila envelope from which Lewis removed some paperwork. I thought, *No way, they really use "the papers" for orders. Just like in the movies!*

He said, "The badges will get you into the facility. Your orders will be given to you by the CO. If, for some reason, he isn't available, hand these papers to the acting CO. The papers should allow them to brief you on why you've been requested." He studied each of us and continued. "This is a training type mission for all of you. We've been told you will not leave the friendly confines of RAM. Do you have any questions?"

I had about a million, but I wanted to get moving so I kept quiet. My stomach was already flip-flopping all over. I needed to get moving before I decided I didn't want to go.

"Okay, pack up and be ready to roll out in thirty minutes."

That was a shocking statement. It was really happening. I was going on a mission to save humanity. If we accomplished the mission, kids would read about me in school books, in a world made safer by me. Or, more likely, I'd be hauling trash for the real heroes of this battle. Yeah, that's more likely how it'll work... another dream dead!

I made my way home double quick to say goodbye to Darline and re-check my kit. Saying goodbye was hard, but not what I had expected. I finally asked her, "What's the deal, chick? I don't expect a hero's send-off, but I anticipated a little more emotion."

She stared at me with wet eyes and said, "Look, this isn't goodbye, it's just a break in the daily routine. If I say goodbye, it feels final, like you're not coming home. Like you might get eaten outside of our little community and I'm not ready for that."

We drew into a long embrace, letting the moment happen. When we pulled away, we clicked back to the business at hand. I opened my bag, checking my Ruger SR 556, CZ P07, XDm, and my S&W Bodyguard in an ankle holster.

Darline was watching me load up and asked, "Why your personal guns? I thought you couldn't wait to play with the big boy toys."

I explained that I'd given it a lot of consideration. Other than the SAW (M249) being used for crowd suppression, I was more comfortable with my guns. The ones I'd been shooting for years. We needed accuracy and shot discipline, not three or more shots for one kill. I still planned to take a few military toys, but I would rely on what had always worked for me and worked well.

She told me, "That's really grown-up of you" – always busting my chops!

CHAPTER 26:
NOT FAST ENOUGH

The Senator tried to figure out how to activate the two-way radio. Apparently the big button on the side had escaped his notice. His thoughts raced back to the days when he had a staff to do these menial tasks for him. Furious and red-faced, he reverted to screaming for Williams.

The door guard entered the room in a panic, ready to fight whatever monsters had made their way into the Senator's office, only to find the Senator seated at his desk with veins bulging in his high forehead.

"You, whatever your name is, get Williams in my office now," he screamed.

The guard, confused by the Senator's reaction, hesitated for a moment. His indecision caused the Senator more distress, and he bellowed, "Get Williams, you idiot!"

The guard about-faced into the hall and grabbed his two-way. "Lieutenant Williams, the Senator wants you in his office. Now! His words, not mine, LT."

Williams closed his eyes and leaned his head back in total frustration. "Let the idiot know I'm on my way."

Minutes later, Williams halted outside the threshold and said, "What?"

The Senator looked up and ordered Williams to enter the office.

"Senator, I'm busy keeping this camp from being overrun. I do not have time to sit. What do you want?"

The Senator, in an uncharacteristic move, dropped the attitude and started talking. "The plan for overrunning RAM is taking too long. We need to move it along and we need to do so now."

Williams pushed down the urge to rush the Senator and remove his head. Instead, he asked, "What do you suggest? I'm not sending more men or equipment than we've already committed. So be creative in your response."

The Senator bristled but again moved forward. "It's time to activate Operation Move In. Make it happen and do so now. Dismissed."

Williams had known this day was coming and he had readied his troops for it. One call would bring them out of standby and launch the plan. He dreaded the action, but it was necessary to meet the objective.

"I'll launch it by EOD, that's end-of-day in case you weren't able to figure it out."

With a sneering grin, the Senator started to rise from his desk. As he prepared to fill the air with his pompous voice, Williams said, "The big button on the side of the talkie thing makes it work. Next time, take two minutes to figure it out. If you'd like, I can have one of the five-year-olds come give you a lesson."

Williams didn't give the senator a chance to retort; he

about-faced and walked away.

"This is LT Williams, launch Operation Move In. I repeat, launch Operation Move In." He looked skyward and asked a God he didn't believe in for forgiveness.

Chapter 27:
A Long Way from Home

When the Humvee pulled up to my house, I grabbed my stuff and kissed Darline. I managed to say, "While I'm gone, I won't be upset if you find a new SUV for me. I'm getting tired of walking everyplace."

She got a glint in her eye that told me I'd made a mistake. I would probably return home to a Big Wheel in the garage. With an evil grin, she pushed me out the door.

As I walked to the Humvee, she yelled, "Randy, make sure my pain-in-the-ass makes it home safe and with all of his parts. I'd ask you to do the same for Lisa, but she can take care of herself."

Lisa opened her door, stuck her head out and bellowed, "I'll keep an eye on all of them. They're only men after all and will inevitably *create* trouble. That's when they'll all start looking for a woman to save them."

Mildly annoyed, Randy reached back from the driver's seat and shut Lisa's door. Then he looked at Darline and nodded his head, telling her we would all make it home… it was an unspoken promise.

I stepped to the passenger side, giving Darline one last

look before entering the Humvee.

After glancing around the cab, I noticed everyone had the same idea. We'd all brought the weapons we were used to, the ones we trusted. The SAW and M107 LRSR would be the only exceptions. Nothing we carried matched the rate of fire of the SAW. It would come in handy if we ended up in a jam. Being the most physically able of the group, Randy would carry the SAW along with his Daniel Defense AR in .308. He tossed the M107 LRSE in the cargo area. We didn't think we'd need it, but Randy really liked it. So, we found the space for it.

Stone carried his Tavor X95, an excellent choice if we would be clearing houses or in close combat situations. He could also drill two-inch holes at two hundred yards all day long. Lisa sported a Sig MPX, a 9mm AR she was deadly accurate with. Will had his Windham Weaponry CDI AR in 5.56. I've never seen him shoot it. But if what he did with the M4 was any indication, he wouldn't be wasting ammunition. He's one-shot, one-kill. Jax was equally as deadly with his Springfield Saint AR in 5.56.

I smiled and said, "Well, looks like we all had the same bad dream about those M4s."

Randy looked over, "Amen, brother, this is the gun I know and trust. And, I feel better with all of you bringing the guns you trust. We need to know that we can rely on each other and it starts with our weapons." He started to say more, but caught himself and just said, "We ready for this?"

"Let's roll," we replied unanimously.

Lewis broke over the radio as we drove through the gate of our community, "This is Lewis, is our MST on the road, over?"

I grabbed the mic and replied, "MST moving out, over."

"Great news, your group call sign is MST1. Your individual calls are your last names. Always respond to any radio traffic that has your call signs. Check in every hour even if you think you're out of range. Someone will pick you up and relay it. Good copy on that, over?"

I clicked over and said, "Good copy, MST1, out." And with that we were off.

We followed the prescribed route and made excellent time. It appeared to be a well-used military route. Abandoned cars were pushed to the side; in some areas large amounts of them lined the roadsides. The military had arranged the cars to form an ad hoc barrier. We speculated it was to keep the UCs off the roads especially in areas where their concentrations were heavy.

Halfway into our trip we hadn't made contact with survivors or UCs. But signs of the war we were fighting were everywhere. From burned-out houses with bullet-riddled cars in front of them to town squares leveled by high explosives. It was like being on a post-apocalyptic movie set.

We could see settlements in the distance, highlighted by guard towers and all manner of barricades. The guard towers became a common theme. We all knew that you must see this enemy before it sees you. Doing so could mean the difference between your community being overrun and living another day. I realized how like-minded the people of RAM were. We will beat this virus back.

It was a relatively quiet ride, but as we took in our surroundings, we started thinking the same thing. So I figured I'd just say it, "How bad are things that they asked a bunch of fifty-plus-year-olds to help get it under control? I mean…"

Lisa cut me off, "Hey, you guys are the old men. I'm still in my thirties and plan on being in much better shape than all of you when I hit fifty."

We were quiet for a second when Jax and Will, in unison, chimed in, "Otto, I'm in my thirties, too."

I was, for some unknown reason, peeved by the gloating. Then, for no good reason, Stone tossed in his two cents, "Otto, you're my older brother by six years, soooo."

I fought back as any old man would, "All right, ladies, keep it down, we need to stay alert."

And for that they rewarded me with snickering from the back… snickering, like little kids. Then Stone broke in."It should be check-in time. Did you forget because of your age and all?"

Son of a… but he was correct. I grabbed the mic and through gritted teeth called in."MST1 checking in, SITREP is all clear."

We didn't get a response, but Lewis said that might

happen.

Stone followed up by continuing my thought. "You do have a point, Otto. It must be getting rough that they're pressing us into service with only two weeks of training. Makes you wonder what's waiting for us at the Entry Point."

Will joined in. "It's not unusual for our military or government to engage with foreign militia, tribes, or even mercenaries for that matter. They understand the terrain, the local politics, and the hiding places of the enemy. It makes good sense, but this, this is something altogether different. I never thought I'd see this day. The day we needed to organize and call the militias into service in our own country."

The word militia stuck in my head. That's basically what we were, a well-organized militia, built from the civilian population. The founding fathers got it right and thank God RAM split and we retained our right to KEEP AND BEAR ARMS. That simple protection of our inherent right might save RAM from this virus and the monsters it created.

The rest of the ride was as uneventful as it had started, albeit cramped in a vehicle designed for a max of five people, but still uneventful. That changed when we picked up I-68 and got closer to the West Virginia border and our destination.

Even from this distance it became obvious that the military machine was operating at full throttle. Black Hawks could be seen coming and going, with some hovering and firing at some unseen enemy on the ground.

Randy stopped the Humvee, and all eyes shifted to him. He looked around and met all of our questioning stares with a hard look. He asked one simple question: "Are you all sure you want to do this? This is our last chance to turn around, go home, and defend our community. It looks like all hell is breaking loose. I don't believe any of us would blame another if they decided to let the pros handle it. I'm still going, but we're under no obligation to lay down our lives on this mission."

The cab fell silent for a full sixty seconds. Randy gave a nod and said, "Okay then, let's go do our part to save this country." And with that, we continued towards our mission.

We rolled up to the gate about forty minutes later, and we really weren't ready for what we saw. The military was engaged in full-on combat operations. Black Hawks flew in and out every thirty seconds, artillery batteries stood ready to unleash hell. The men, women, and machines of war moved in every direction.

We were about three miles from the entry point, and it was obvious the focus was on that single point of entry. We could hear occasional full-auto small-arms fire as well as large explosions. The realization that RAM truly was at war smacked us in the face.

Will leaned forward and said, "Let me handle the gate access. With what I'm seeing, tensions will be high, and we don't want to get shot by some jumpy pimple-faced kid."

We agreed and came to a stop. A Bradley, positioned immediately in front of the other side of the double gate, greeted us. Two machinegun nests on the ground and two more in towers flanked the gate on either side. They trained every single weapon on our vehicle.

With the late morning sun shining directly into the front windshield, we couldn't make out any of the soldiers' faces. But that didn't matter. The destructive force pointing in our direction was all we needed to see. Will opened his door as a voice broke over a loudspeaker.

"You've approached a restricted zone. State your business."

Will shut the door behind him and shouted, "We are call sign MST1, sent by request of RAM 1st Division out of Cleveland. We have access badges and papers; we are to report to the CO for further instruction."

The hatch of the Bradley opened and, you guessed it, a pimple-faced kid popped up. He was, however, a large kid with a very serious look on his face. He told Will to stay put and ordered someone named Adams to approach the small access port that was built into the fence.

Adams approached, opened the access port, which amounted to an eight-inch by eight-inch hinged steel plate with a padlock holding it shut. He stepped back about three feet, bringing his M4 to his shoulder at the same time. The kid in the Bradley directed Will to get all of our badges and drop them through the port and then back three feet away from it. Will came to the Humvee and collected our badges. We asked him if it was a good idea to surrender them, but he didn't respond. He immediately took them to the port and did as directed. The soldier named Adams picked them up and ran them to the Bradley.

The young soldier in the Bradley looked over each badge carefully and read every word on the papers. He grabbed his shoulder mic and spoke into it. About thirty seconds later, he motioned for Adams to open the gate.

Will re-entered our vehicle and said, "You're welcome."

I asked, "Why didn't you respond when we asked about turning over our badges and paperwork?"

"We have a Bradley and four machine guns trained on us. With tensions high, I wasn't going to give them the impression we were planning something. I wanted to get the information to them without having holes put in my body." I had to agree with that logic.

The first gate slid open, and we pulled in and stopped in front of the second gate. The gate shut behind us and they ordered us out of the Humvee for a virus inspection. Adams, this time accompanied by a young female soldier named Vasquez, made their way over to us as we lined up along the driver's side of our Humvee.

Vasquez remained about ten feet away with her M4 at the high ready position. Adams approached with what appeared to be a small, palm-sized medical kit. He unzipped it and produced cotton swabs and six clear, liquid-filled vials. He set them down on the hood and told each of us to swab the inside of our mouth, insert it into a vial then step away.

One by one we did as directed, and one by one nothing happened to the liquid in the vials. Adams yelled to the Bradley, "All clear, Hawkins, no sign of infection."

Now the Bradley commander had a name, but it didn't make him any more personable. He yelled out, "All clear. MST1, proceed to the TOC by following I-68 to Casteel to Sky View. Colonel Watts is expecting you in five minutes."

With that, he dismissed us and sent us on our way. The surrounding activity felt reassuring that we still had a functioning military and alarming that the military was in full combat mode on our own soil. The sight had the inside of the Humvee quiet for the entire ride.

We made it to the TOC (Tactical Operations Center) in under four minutes. A young lady, whose uniform was immaculate, greeted us as we exited our Humvee. The well-dressed young lady introduced herself as Master Sergeant Lucas, and she was all business. She didn't wait for us to introduce ourselves, just directed us to follow her and turned on her heel.

This whole helping the military save the world thing was starting to make me uncomfortable. I couldn't shake the feeling they were keeping something from us. Which would make me crazy. Just like Randy's bag or the M939s.

215

I needed the information they had. But, because no humor crossed MS Lucas' face, or really any sign of her being a nice person, I stuffed my crazy urge for now.

But one of my questions needed to be answered, so I asked her as we walked at a quick pace, "The test we took at the gate, can we get any of those kits for our community? How dependable are they?"

MS Lucas slammed to a stop and turned to face me. She appeared unreasonably annoyed with me, almost like Darline, only meaner.

"What's your name?" she asked.

"Hammer, Otto Hammer."

A slight smirk crossed her face but disappeared as fast as it appeared, something I've grown accustomed to over the years. "Mr. Hammer, you will hold your questions until you are in the TOC with Colonel Watts."

She began turning away when I blurted out, "Why are you so..."

MS Lucas snapped back and appeared within an inch of my face before I could blink. "Why am I so what, Mr. Hammer? Please finish your question, since it is obvious you don't take direction well." She had literally scared the question directly out of my head.

I just stood there staring into her bloodshot eyes that looked like they hurt and said, "I forgot."

She snapped back around and continued walking towards the TOC entrance. Randy leaned in and asked me, "Otto, what in the name of all things holy is wrong with you?"

I started to answer when he said loudly, "Otto, it was more of a statement than a question. Now please be quiet."

We entered the TOC and were led to the Colonel's office. MS Lucas knocked and entered almost simultaneously. Colonel Watts was standing in front of a large map of Entry Point One via a satellite view. Several other men and women crowded around the map with him.

I started to think we were in way over our heads. This was a military operation, and they didn't appear to need any assistance from poorly trained civilians.

The Colonel glanced over and dismissed MS Lucas. He stood about six feet and appeared every part the soldier you'd want defending the country. But something struck me as odd. The group of officers each wore ACUs with a side arm holstered. It was wartime in a war zone and somehow I had ended up in the middle of it.

The Colonel didn't mince words. He walked to a small table, picked up a folder, read something on the inside jacket, and looked up at us. "I think this is a bad idea. Not because I don't admire your willingness to defend your country. But because you don't have enough training and I don't wish to waste resources pulling your asses out of a jam." He continued, "You're going to Terra Alta, West Virginia, and you're leaving in less than ten minutes. We have a report that survivors may be in the area. Satellite images spotted a large sign in a field that reads HELP. The sign wasn't there three weeks ago during the last drone sweep of Terra Alta. The area appeared to be clear of UCs and with the threat intensifying at our gate, we consider this low priority. That's why you're here. Go to Terra Alta, assess the situation, call in a report and relay the message we give you to whoever you find. You'll find this information in the folder. The folder will travel with you."

After a brief pause during which he made eye contact with each of us, he said, "Engage and eliminate any UC you encounter during your recon. You'll be issued UC testing kits, which you are to use on any living you encounter. If the kit displays purple, the person is infected and will need to be eliminated. If it remains clear, the person is not infected. Full directions are in the kits. Read them on your way to Terra Alta." He paused about one half of a second and asked, "Any questions?" Then immediately he said, "Excellent, dismissed and good luck." He turned back to the map.

I expected more, and I think the others did as well. We stood waiting for something to happen. After an awkward thirty seconds, MS Lucas came back in, spreading her own form of happy, and escorted us out of the TOC and back to our Humvee.

She handed us our orders then handed each of us five kits with twenty tests in each kit and turned away. Stopping short, she kept her back to us and said, "One thing missing from your briefing. We've started to take live fire from the other side of the wall. If you are fired on, fire back. This war is escalating." She then continued back to the TOC and disappeared behind its doors.

CHAPTER 28:
APPLYING OUR LEARNING

As we drove back to Sky View Drive we got a closer look at the converted housing units. The former prison made an excellent choice for housing refugees. It looked like it had a good number of survivors already living behind its fences.

"Well, that went as I expected," I said. "I have to tell you, I'm feeling like part of the team now."

After a few seconds, we started to laugh. It helped break up the tension. But our smiles faded as we rounded what looked like a cargo center at the high point of the area. We had a clear view of I-68 and Right Entry Point One.

What we saw was stunning. RAM troops were trying to defend what looked like an endless line of cars and trucks and thousands of people on foot. All of them trying to enter RAM through the entry point.

Will summed it up when he uttered, "What the f...."

As he trailed off, the magnitude of the situation came into full view. RAM soldiers had built fencing that started on either side of the entry point main gate. Not as a deterrent to entry, but to provide cover for those waiting in line to enter RAM from BSU. The fencing formed an arched cage to protect hundreds of people from the UC masses drawn to the activity. Anyone caught outside of the cage would be dragged to the ground and eaten.

The scene came straight out of a horror movie. RAM Black Hawks and AH-64 Apaches swarmed thick in the sky above the cage. They laid down covering fire at the front of the entrance to the caged area. Soldiers on raised-steel platforms provided close-in fire support. So many people, living and UC, had been caught in the hailstorm of bullets that even from our position we could see the ground was stained red with blood. The solders on the platforms tried to administer the virus test to the people that managed to find safety inside the cage.

Will spoke first and said what we were all thinking, "If one infected person gets inside that cage, it'll be a massacre. The soldiers will be forced to kill them all. I can't watch this. Otto, get this thing rolling."

I hit the gas a little harder than I planned to. The wheels of the Humvee chirped in response. Every soldier in earshot turned in our direction, some bringing weapons to high ready. Just another indicator of the highly charged atmosphere. I gave a quick wave to let them know we were not a threat and continued down Sky View Drive toward our objective.

As we crossed over I-68, we noticed a grouping of heavy equipment vehicles being worked on. The bulldozers, earthmovers, and enormous dump trucks were getting thick tubular steel bars welded to the cabs. Razor wire was linked between the bars, forming a glistening spider web of death. They appeared to be preparing to enter the heart of the UC mass. *That's going to be the worst job in the history of time*, I thought as we continued past them.

We finished crossing I-68 and picked up Route 5 South on our way to Terra Alta. The mood was not one of levity or anticipation. We were still in shock by what we had witnessed. And the thirty-eight-minute ride wasn't going to shake those images from our minds.

I finally said, "This is the last time we travel this far away from home, no matter the reason. I'm not comfortable at all with being here after seeing what's happening at the Entry Point."

Everyone agreed almost immediately.

We had been on Brandonville Pike Road for about four miles when Randy, now in the passenger seat, asked me to stop. He became a little impatient when he noticed the questioning look on my face.

"Otto, just stop driving. Now works best."

I slowed to a stop in the middle of the road. Randy jumped out and ran to the cargo area of the Humvee and grabbed his bag. After about thirty seconds he got back in the cab and started handing out the cut-resistant sleeves we'd used when clearing the Hicks' house.

He directed all of us to put them on under the heavy fabric of the ACU we were wearing. He didn't ask us, he told us to do it and said, "We are all going home after this. If you don't believe that to be true, please stay in the Humvee.

I'm not losing any friends on this cluster fuck of a mission. Also, I don't think we should split into teams unless forced to. Got it? Good. Let's do this and get home."

We drove another mile and came upon a purpose-built roadblock at the intersection with Sanders Street. It consisted of abandoned cars, earth-packed mounds, and pikes. The latter of which were placed at head height with several UCs hanging limp from their sharpened ends. The UCs were severely decomposed, making us question how long it had been since anyone had manned the roadblock.

The roadblock was extensive and well-built. It incorporated homes on each of the corners of the intersection, extending out from that point. The only open area was our current location. We considered going around it but noticed what looked like tank trap barriers with razor wire strung between them encompassing the perimeter of the small city.

After waiting several minutes for the guards to make contact, we realized the roadblock had been abandoned, so we exited the Humvee. After several more minutes with no activity, we probed the roadblock for an entrance. If a vehicle entrance was part of the main roadblock, it wasn't something we could easily see. After more probing, we determined that no vehicles would have had access through the barrier. Only living beings would've been able to pass.

Will pulled out the satellite images and determined that a vehicle entrance to the city was about a quarter mile to the east. He also determined that we were very close, about five hundred yards, from the HELP sign's location.

Will said, "Let's gear up and search the area on foot."

I agreed. It would be a much faster option when compared to searching for another entrance. Assuming it was clear of UCs or hostile humans, we'd be forced to backtrack through town when we could cover the five hundred yards in about ten minutes.

The HELP sign was set up just outside of a small wooded area. We assumed that the person or persons who'd made it would be close by. All that stood in our way was getting through one of the homes blocking our path.

We chose the only house without boarded-up windows or doors. Will called it.

"Let's stack up two on the left, one on the right. I'll take the breach position. Randy and Otto will remain back in case we run into trouble."

Jax and Lisa moved left while Stone went right, and Will started his countdown.

"3… 2… 1!" And with that, Will kicked the door nearly off its hinges. Lisa, Stone, then Jax entered immediately. Each converged on a different area of the home. All checked in as clear within three minutes. The house, however, was anything but clear. It had been the scene of a vicious battle for life with no clear victor. The stench of rotting flesh hung thick in the air, and the source became nightmarishly clear.

The main room of the small four-room house held seven dead bodies. From the smell, the wall of flies and amount of decay, it appeared they had been rotting for weeks, possibly months.

On closer inspection it appeared all had suffered head trauma, but it was hard to tell how many, if any, had been infected. Our guess was that someone turned, a fight broke out, and they all ended up infected. We found no reason to stay in the house to investigate. They were dead; it's as simple as that. So we exited through the back door and advanced towards our target.

Stone said something we were all thinking, "Things are going way too smoothly. I don't like it. Maybe I shouldn't question it, but I have a sense this is going to blow up any second. Nothing has been easy for the last couple of months, so getting this close to the Entry Point and having nothing happen? I've got a bad feeling."

I felt the same but wanted to keep our mood light, so I spoke the following words... out loud, "I understand how you feel, but look on the bright side. We're outside on a beautiful day in a great area of our country helping our military hold the line."

Every eye locked on me when I finished talking, and I think I hated myself after saying it. I was new to leading people into life-threatening situations and apparently saying stupid things is a nervous habit of mine.

Lisa said, "What in the actual Hell are you talking about, Otto? Are you okay? Has the stress finally broken that pea-sized man-brain of yours?"

I could only respond in my best squad leader voice

with, "Keep moving, people."

We had traveled about two hundred yards when we sensed something was wrong. Stone was dead on when he said it would blow up. Standing in the middle of this large flat field, with no cover to speak of, made us perfect targets. I started to register all the places a group of UCs could hide, and it made my stomach rumble. Suddenly, the ground in front of me exploded at the same time Stone let out a sharp yelp of pain and grabbed the side of his head. Then another explosion to the left of Jax, and finally the sound of gunshots confirmed we were under fire!

Will yelled, "Spread out and run, head for the tree line."

The tree line started about one hundred yards away and I worried we were running directly at the person or persons firing on us.

"Will, why the tree line? What direction are the shots coming from?"

He replied, "I see two people waving at us from the trees and that tells me we're headed the right way."

I looked again and spotted the two people he was talking about. The ground exploded several more times as we zigged and zagged toward cover while trying to avoid being shot. I yelled out to Stone, "Are you okay? That looks like a good amount of blood coming from your head."

He replied, "I think it's only a flesh wound. But if I get that SOB in my sights, I'm putting him down. He's obviously a terrible shot and if he shot my ear off, I'll shoot him twice after he's dead."

I realized at that point how hard it is to run when you're laughing.

As we neared the tree line, I did a quick head count and came up one head short. My heart sank when I realized Randy was MIA. Stopping hard and spinning to scan the area behind us saved my life. At the very second I stopped, another round hit directly in front of me. The impact sent me diving to my right where I used the tall grass, mere feet from the tree line, as cover.

When I poked my head up, I spotted the end of a rifle barrel, twenty yards away, jutting out of the tall grass. Suddenly it jerked twice followed by a muzzle flash each time. While I waited for Randy to stand, gunfire erupted behind me. I turned to find the entire team with their weapons trained on a small hill about three hundred yards to the east. The earth on the hillside was jumping from the impacts of the teams' return fire.

I noticed one body on the ground already then a second rolled out from behind some scrub to the left of the lifeless body. Will called a ceasefire, bringing a deafening silence with it. Holding our positions for about half a minute, we began to move after the two people in the tree line started jabbering.

They blathered on about the UCs and how they needed help to get away from them. That they needed to be taken someplace safe, and we NEEDED to take them someplace safe.

The tone of that last comment gave us pause and angered me into action. "Shut up and answer the following questions without hesitation or you get to stay here."

"But… but…," they interrupted as they choked back tears.

I shut them down. "I told you both to shut up and answer my questions. Now hold it together. I'll try to make it simple for you."

They sucked it up and nodded. I was being hard on them, but I had a suspicion they didn't belong here. The trembling, the crying, the basic sticks and whatnot they had for weapons, it *smelled* wrong to me.

"Okay, that's better. Is that your sign in the field?"

They nodded.

"Can you tell us who shot at us?"

They shook their heads.

"How did you get here?"

No response.

"That's what I thought. We need to determine if we have a breach in the wall. How did you enter RAM and end up in Terra Alta?"

Again, nothing from either of them, just blank water-filled eyes staring back at me.

The sickly skinny young man looked up and said, "I'm thirsty; I need some of your water."

I almost punched him for two reasons. First, he was only worried about himself, not his companion. The second being the way he asked. His phrasing was all wrong. His attitude was, *I had what he needed, and that meant I should give him some.* All of our heads shot in his direction when he said that. We realized what it meant: They were BSU.

I tossed the water at him, just as Stone let loose with a string of obscenities. He had slapped some antibacterial ointment and a large band aid on his ear. The bullet had clipped the outside of the top of his earlobe and took a good amount of skin with it. It wasn't a critical injury, but it looked painful.

I walked over to check on him and discovered he was swearing about more than his ear. I followed his gaze and joined in the obscenity parade. About twenty UCs were heading our way from the area of the roadblock. The gunfire must have drawn them out, and they had a bead on us. We possessed enough firepower to take care of them until the second, much larger, wave joined them, completely cutting us off from our planned exit point.

Some rustling in the trees behind us signaled that we had allowed ourselves to get flanked on two sides.

Randy yelled, "Let's move, people, we have some company that wants to eat us."

We took off like a shot toward the small city center of Terra Alta.

While running across the field, I yelled to Jax to radio for extraction and looked over my left shoulder to see he already had the radio out.

He yelled back, "I have nothing but squelch coming from the radio. What's that mean?"

Will joined in. "It means we're getting interference. Did they go over what to do in situations like this?"

"Will, you're the only one of us with military training. Why are you asking us that question? Don't you know a workaround?" I asked.

Will sounded exasperated when he replied, "Otto, I'm not trained on that style radio; it's a networking handheld radio."

Well shit, was what I was thinking. I may have said it out loud, but it didn't matter at this point if I did. We were quickly getting surrounded. The group we'd heard in the trees emerged and it was a good-sized crowd of nastiness. The mass cutting us off from our vehicle was now in full pursuit and spreading out in a long perimeter.

Will yelled, "Let's try to circle back to the Hummer through the section that's razor wired off. If we can find a board, we can lay it over and walk across. But we'll need to put some distance between us and the UC so pick up the pace."

I've mentioned I'm not a youngster, and I had already hit full speed. My backpack, although not enormous, weighed me down. I wasn't going to be able to pick up the pace.

"Will, I won't be able to do that. I'm already sucking wind." I yelled to Randy, "Pull the SAW around and get ready."

He seemed to anticipate my next move and got it ready to go immediately and yelled, "Ready when you are."

I screamed, "Will, keep everyone else running! We'll only be a few seconds behind you. Randy, NOW."

We stopped and turned as the refugees, Lisa, Jax, then Stone and Will passed us.

We hit the ground and opened up on the UC mass. Aiming low, we shot hips and legs to slow as many of them down as possible. The first two rows collapsed in a heap, tangling with the ones that followed and slowing the advance of the herd. Blood and body parts sprayed in every direction as Randy laid down an unrelenting string of fire. He burned through the ammo pouch in a matter of seconds and we were on the move again. We had bought ourselves several valuable minutes, and we needed every one of them.

We looked back just as Will took a hard left, not the direction we needed. I got confused for a second, then noticed a group of UCs pouring out of the building in the direction we needed. This had gone sideways fast.

We caught up with the group and formed a loose perimeter. The refugees ended up in the middle. It was at this point that we turned into the small downtown area of Terra Alta. I asked no one in particular, "Why did they tell us that the town was clear of UC when CLEARLY it isn't?"

Will answered, "They used drones for the recon. These things all came out from cover. They wouldn't have seen them. And if they were using FLIR, it wouldn't have picked them up because they're cold, no heat signature.

Plus, the INTEL is old. Things can change quickly in a matter of days."

The answer didn't help my mood, but it made sense. I hate these things!

Within a few minutes, we'd lost the BSU refugees and ended up in this basement. Surrounded by stinky food. We have no contact with the military in Hazelton, no contact with home, and no plan to escape this mess.

The apocalypse wasn't going how I'd planned. Not at all.

This is Call Sign MST1 over and out... for now.

Continued in
Of Patriots and Tyrants
The Divided America Zombie Apocalypse

Thanks for reading! I'd like to thank all of my friends and family for their support. This book is the result of a promise I made to myself and, with the help of so many people, I kept that promise!

Reviews are valuable to independent writers. Please consider leaving yours where you purchased this book. Feel free to like me on Facebook at B.D. Lutz/Autor Page. You'll be the first notified of specials and new releases. You can email me at: CLELUTZ11@gmail.com.

No matter what life throws at you, FIGHT LIKE THE THIRD MONKEY!

ABOUT THE AUTHOR

Hello! I'm supposed to tell you a little about myself, so here we go. I bet you can't wait! I was born in Cleveland Ohio. I now live in NEO (North East Ohio) with my wonderful wife (she told me to say that). Our beautiful daughter lives in California with her extraordinary husband, and we miss them every day.

In my early adult life I spent time as a Repo-Man for a rent to own furniture company, a bill collector and heavy drinker. Then, I pulled myself together and spent twenty-seven years working my way through sales management in corporate America. However, one day, I was sitting in a meeting and the right person said the right thing at the right time and I realized enough was truly enough. I've always wanted to do this, write a book, and I realized that we, you and me, have about fifteen minutes on the face of this planet and I needed to do one of the things I had always wanted to do. And, well, this is it.

If you're wondering, yes, I'm a conservative, I own guns, and I hate paying taxes.

My hope is that one day you're sitting in a meeting, delivering a package, serving someone dinner, or doing whatever it is you do for a living and decide that enough is enough. It's the scariest thing you'll ever do. But I promise at no point in your life will you feel more alive than the day you take control of the life you're living!